The Oil Prince

Kate Goldman

The Oil Prince

Published by Kate Goldman

Copyright © 2019 by Kate Goldman

ISBN 978-1-07441-330-9

First printing, 2019

www.KateGoldmanBooks.com

PRINTED IN THE UNITED STATES OF AMERICA

Dedication

 I want to dedicate this book to my beloved husband, who makes every day in my life worthwhile. Thank you for believing in me when nobody else does, giving me encouragement when I need it the most, and loving me simply for being myself.

Table of Contents

Chapter 1

"Hey! Jerk!" Emily screamed after a car that had just driven over a puddle and splashed her. The driver did not even stop. She watched the car until it disappeared. She was annoyed that the driver did not even pull up to check that she was fine. Emily was just on her way back home after having gone for a walk on a Sunday afternoon. She looked down at her jeans, they were soaked. She growled and tried to wipe them with her hands but it was of no use. She sighed and just started walking again.

She walked down the street and turned around a corner, quickening her pace to get home earlier. As she was passing the gas station on the corner, she started contemplating going into the convenience store to pick up a few items. Then she remembered her dirty, wet jeans and thought about how bad she must look in them. As she approached the shop, she saw a parked Bentley. She recognized the last digits on the license plate, it was the same car that had driven over the puddle earlier.

There was a man leaning against the car. He was wearing a white shirt and a pair of black trousers. He had caramel-colored skin, dark eyebrows, a straight medium-sized nose, a well-trimmed beard, and jet-black hair. He was looking at his phone. Emily quickly approached him. "Excuse me," she said.

He had dark eyes and a cold stare. "Can I help you with something?" he asked Emily. His voice was deep and cold. It sent shivers down her spine.

"Yes," Emily replied. "Earlier you drove over a puddle and it splashed me." His eyes dropped to the obvious wet patch on her jeans and back up to her face. She was not very tall. Her skin was a nice caramel color. She had very curly light brown coils of hair tied up into a messy bun. She had brown eyes and medium-sized lips.

"So do you want money for dry cleaning?" he asked her. He did not really understand what her point was. Either way, she needed the money to dress a little bit more elegantly. Even if she had not been splashed by the water, she was still dressed untidily. She hadn't even brushed her hair.

Emily frowned at him. He was quite rude. "A simple apology would be fine," she snapped.

"Apology?" He raised his eyebrows. He was definitely not going to apologize. He was not used to doing so, and he never really had to.

"Yes, an apology."

He put his hand in his pocket and fished out his wallet. He pulled out a few hundred dollars and attempted to give them to Emily. She looked at his hand and laughed sarcastically. *So he is one of those arrogant rich men,* Emily thought to herself.

"I do not want your money," she said to him.

"Not enough?" he asked and fished out more money.

"I don't want your money!" Emily raised her voice. It was so insulting, and she could not understand why he was behaving that way. "Why can't you just apologize like a normal person?" she asked.

"Did you not come here to be compensated?" he asked.

"No, I did not."

He scanned her body from head to toe. "You could use the money. Your wardrobe is in need of assistance," he said to her. Her dress sense was not up to par. He was used to seeing women dressed better than that.

"Excuse me? You have not even seen my wardrobe."

"I have seen enough," he said with a slight frown on his face.

"Don't insult me." Emily placed her hands on her hips.

"I was not insulting you."

"People like you are a waste of time."

"People like me?"

"Yes! You rich people think that you are above everyone else. I am just wasting my breath here."

Emily rolled her eyes and walked off. There was no point in arguing with him. It seemed that he was not going to apologize to her.

The man just shrugged his shoulders and watched her walking away. He went through life not having to apologize for anything. He was the way he was. It surprised him that she had not taken the money from him. After all, that was what most people wanted from him anyway, minimum-wage earning people were easily bought. All he had to do was wave a few dollar bills at them and they would do whatever he wanted them to do.

On Monday Emily went to the office of the company where she worked after attending several meetings in the morning. "Hi, Rachel," Emily greeted the receptionist on her way in.

"Hello, Emily," the receptionist replied. "Prince Fady asked that you see him as soon as you arrived," she added. Emily gave Rachel a questioning look.

"Does he want a report or something?"

"I am not sure what the reason is."

"Okay." Emily quickly dashed into her office to drop off her bag and then she headed to Prince Fady's office. His secretary greeted her when she arrived and escorted her in. Emily bowed her head to the sheikh. "Good afternoon, Prince Fady," she said to him.

Prince Fady was a prince of a Middle Eastern country called Al-Bisha. He was the second eldest son. There were four boys and two girls in total. His family owned an oil company and they had extended their business to the U.S. Their branch in Dallas was responsible for receiving their imported oil from Al-Bisha and then selling it to some U.S. companies from Dallas. They also had a few oilfields in Dallas and Houston, and a refinery in Dallas. Prince Fady had been managing the Dallas branch. His role included meeting with business partners, inspecting the imported oil, and recruiting the engineers and geophysicists. He was very hands-on with his work. He was quite meticulous. Emily had been working for him for just two years and in that time, she had quickly gained his recognition due to her hard work and intelligent ideas.

"Miss Gibson, come in." Sheikh Fady smiled at Emily. The sheikh was sitting on one of the sofas in his office.

"You wanted to—" Before Emily could finish speaking, she noticed that there was another man sitting across from the sheikh. He was dressed in navy blue trousers and a white shirt. He was looking down at his phone. She gasped when she recognized him. "Oh my," she said.

"What is the matter?" the sheikh asked her.

"Your guest, I've met him before."

"Really?" the sheikh asked. "Basil, do you know her?" he asked the man. The man looked up and saw Emily standing there. He frowned, he recognized her from the previous day. She looked at him with the same displeased expression. At least this time she was dressed well and her hair was brushed.

"I do not. I just met her yesterday," Basil replied.

"Come join us," the sheikh said to Emily. She reluctantly went to join them. "It is good that the two of you have already met," he added.

"Why? Who is she?" Basil asked. He put his phone down.

"This is Emily. She is one of the petrophysicists."

"She works here?"

"Yes."

"As a petrophysicist?" He couldn't believe that Emily was one of the people that analyzed the physical properties of rocks and land before drilling. It was the petrophysicists who concluded whether to drill and how to proceed. He could not see Emily doing that kind of job.

"Yes."

Basil grunted. He was very shocked. He would have expected her to work at some retail shop as a counter service assistant or in an office as a secretary. Emily could hear the judgment in his voice. Clearly he was surprised. She narrowed her gaze at him and wanted to swear at him but she could not, since her boss was sitting right there. She also wanted to let him know that she had a master's in geophysics and had graduated at the top of her class.

"Emily, this is my younger brother, Basil," Sheikh Fady said. Her eyes flew open.

"Brother?" she asked.

"Yes, and he will be around for a while. I will get to the point. We have the opportunity to work with Magenta Oils. I would like to us to supply methane to them. This gives us an opportunity to expand into the methane business. Basil is going to be in charge of this project and I need you to work with him."

Emily had a thousand questions running through her mind. At first she thought that it was great that they were going to work with Magenta Oils. It was one of the biggest oil companies in America. "Me?" she asked. The second thing that went through her mind was the fact that she was going to work with Basil. She did not want to work with Basil.

"Yes."

"No," Basil said. He did not want to work with Emily, either. His father the king had sent him to Dallas because he was so sick of Basil not working at the family company and being irresponsible. He was always getting in trouble, and it was reflecting badly on the royal family. The king had warned him many times but Basil did not listen. So the king wanted to revoke his title as prince and cut off all his finances, but Fady had suggested that Basil work with him in Dallas on this new project. The king agreed. If Basil failed or refused, then he would have his title revoked. Basil had no choice but to comply.

Chapter 2

Fady raised his eyebrows when Basil said no. "Basil?" Fady said.

"Must I work with her?" Basil asked. Fady was not surprised that Basil spoke his mind. His younger brother never held back his thoughts. What surprised Fady was the fact that he did not want to work with Emily. He wondered what transpired when they met, that made his brother not want to work with her.

"Yes, I chose her because she is the best."

Emily looked surprised, but pleased. She felt warm inside after hearing Fady's words. He was the boss but they did not work together that often. They had worked together on a couple of projects and he approved of her work, he said things like "good job" or "good" but he never called her the best. Emily had a small smile on her face. It quickly faded when Basil responded to Fady.

"Really?" he asked sardonically.

"Yes. So I need the two of you to work together," Fady replied. He wanted Emily to work with his brother because he had seen her work, she was highly organized, very intelligent, and good at her job. He could see that she had the potential to progress even further.

Basil sighed. "How will this work?" he asked.

"My assistant is printing out the paperwork. I will have her give both of you copies, and then the two of you can start the planning and decide how you want to start. I will provide you with a team to work with."

"What kind of paperwork?" Basil asked.

"Details about the land, budget, the workers, everything regarding the project."

"How long will it be for?" Emily asked.

"We have three months to provide 200 barrels," Fady replied. Emily's eyes widened.

"It is a bit much," Emily replied. They hadn't even started drilling yet. It was hard to know if the land would produce 200 barrels, and they only had three months to produce that amount. Emily could foresee a bumpy couple of months ahead.

"Yes, it is. I suppose that they have other suppliers approaching them. Can you handle this project?"

"Yes, I can, your highness." Emily always loved to challenge herself when it came to her work. She never gave up on a project without trying.

"Good. You may return to your work," said Fady.

Emily got up and left the room. She was full of mixed emotions. She was excited to have an opportunity to gain new experience. However time was limited, and they were dealing with a big company. The pressure was definitely on. Because of her initial meeting with Basil, she was not keen on him. He was not polite. She did not want to work with him but she did not have a choice.

"So how did you and Miss Gibson meet?" Fady asked Basil after Emily had left the room. Basil sighed furiously before he replied. "It could not have been that bad," Fady added.

"It was that bad," Basil said.

"What happened?"

Basil narrated the incident back to his brother. He was still not pleased about it. Back in Al-Bisha, no woman would ever speak to him like that. Fady laughed a little as he listened to his brother speaking. "She was not that bad," Fady said.

"Is that you being humorous? I did not appreciate her speaking to me like that. She should have just taken the money and left."

"You should have just apologized."

Basil frowned at Fady. "I was not the one driving," he said.

"She did not know that," Fady replied.

"That is not my fault."

"It partially is. You cannot just offer money to people like that and insult their dress sense in the same token." Fady found the situation a little bit amusing. He would have never pegged Emily as a feisty woman but then again his brother's impudence was to blame for her reaction.

"Her wardrobe needed assistance. Do I really have to work with her?" Basil asked.

"Yes, you will have to. Just keep it professional. It will only be for three months. Besides, she is not that bad to work with."

Basil sighed. "Are you confident that this will work? Three months is not a long time," he voiced his concern to his brother. Basil had no choice but to get this project completed, it was better than losing his title. However he was still worried about the project.

"Yes, I am confident. You can do it," Fady replied. He could see potential in his younger brother. He had a PhD in engineering. Basil was very intelligent but he was lazy. He was not interested in working for the family company. After he graduated, he never used his degree. He spent his days either in his villa or on a yacht partying and traveling.

***

Two days later, Emily and Basil had to go see the land they were going to drill. They both had had the opportunity to read over the paperwork Fady had prepared for them. They went to the field in separate cars. Basil had his driver drive him there. Emily drove herself there. She arrived a few moments after Basil.

She got out of the car and walked over to where he was standing.

"Good afternoon," Emily greeted Basil when she approached him. She wondered if she was to refer to him as "sir" or "your highness." He was holding his phone and texting.

"You're here," he responded coldly. To him, his tone was natural but to Emily, it was cold.

"I am," she replied. She did not know how else to respond to him. She hated that he was standing there looking at his phone and had not looked at her when she greeted him. The first and second time she met him, he had been on his phone. She wondered what so important that he could not tear himself away from. "We have engineers coming here to meet us. Shall we look around first?" she asked him.

"There is nothing but land here. What is there to see?" Basil replied. Emily frowned. It sounded as though he did not care.

"I will go look," she said.

"Suit yourself," he replied without lifting his head. He was so focused on his phone. Emily rolled her eyes and walked off.

Chapter 3

Emily strolled as she looked at the field. The field was not that big but it was big enough. It was what was underneath that mattered. The land was neat, there were no rocks or grass. This meant that they would be able to drill quicker with no obstacles. The engineers arrived on time. Emily did not have to wait for too long. There were three engineers and a geophysicist, and they arrived in the same car. They got out and approached Emily.

"Good afternoon, Miss Gibson," one of the engineers greeted Emily as he extended his hand to her for a handshake.

"Hello," Emily said as she shook his hand. He introduced himself as Mr. Lyons. He was the head of the engineers. While he was speaking to Emily, she could not help but wonder why Basil was not standing next to her, greeting the engineers also. When she turned her head, she saw him walking towards them. He looked so relaxed and not bothered with what was going on. He had not rushed towards the engineers when they had arrived.

When Basil approached them, he stood beside Emily with one hand in his pocket. Emily was already annoyed by his lack of professionalism. "This is

Prince Basil Tadros," Emily quickly introduced him to the engineers. The four men looked at Basil and bowed their heads to him.

"It's good to meet you, your highness," Mr. Lyons said. Basil just nodded. He looked so uninterested, Emily wanted to smack some sense into him.

"So what do we need to discuss?" Basil asked. It was going to take some time for Basil to adjust to everything. He was not used to attending meetings and having an office. He was never involved in the family business and he had no interest in it. So he just wanted to hurry the process up.

"Mr. Lyons, we want to drill this land for methane," Emily began. After all, the engineers relied on the geophysicist and the petrophysicist to direct the drilling. They were the ones who would study the land and do their calculations, and then work with the engineers on a plan to drill.

Emily explained that they needed to drill for 200 barrels within three months. The four men looked surprised. They stared at Emily in disbelief. "I know the time is short but we have to get it done," Emily said. Even she was still shocked about the timeline. She did not know why it was so short. There was so much to do in just three months.

Mr. Lyons told Emily and Basil that since the timeline was short, they would need to start drilling in two weeks. So that meant that the geophysicist and petrophysicist had two weeks to analyze the soil samples. Emily nervously smiled and told the engineers that they could get it done, even though she was not entirely sure.

Emily felt relieved when the meeting was finished. She was glad that the engineers seemed to be up for the challenge. Most people would have been nervous about the time scale. As she and Basil returned to their cars, she asked him, "Do you think that went well?" since he had not said much. He had only asked two questions, what they were going to discuss and whether they could get the job done. Other than that he had not said much.

"I guess," he replied plainly.

"I mean you were rather quiet." Emily was treading carefully since he was her boss's brother. So she had to pick her words wisely. Basil responded with a grunt and just quickened his pace. He just disliked Emily and did not want to talk too much to her. He also felt like she was going to question him and he did not want that.

Emily watched Basil walking away with her jaw hung open. She could not believe his attitude. He really did not care about the project. It annoyed her. Maybe it was because he was a prince, he did not care about anything other than himself. That being said, he was so different from his brother. Fady was much more professional. He cared about his work and he communicated with his staff. Emily could not understand why it was Basil she had to work with. She just sighed and got into her car. Basil had gotten into his also. They headed their separate ways.

The next morning, Emily was in her office working when Fady came in. Emily stood up from her desk immediately. "Good morning, your highness," she greeted him. She gave him a small bow.

"Morning, Miss Gibson," he replied. His voice and presence were so regal.

"What can I do for you?"

"Come with me."

Emily walked around her desk and approached Fady. "Where are we going?" she asked him. Fady opened the door for Emily and gestured for her to walk out first. "Thank you," she said and walked out of her office.

"I have a new office ready for you and my brother to work in for this project," said Fady. *What?* Emily's subconscious screamed out. She was going to share an office with Basil for the duration of the project? She could not believe it. She liked having her own office.

"A new office for us?" she asked. She did not know what else to say. She did not want to express her displeasure to the boss.

"Yes, I figured that it would make it easier for the two of you to communicate and get the work done." Fady knew that Basil was not going to like the idea of sharing an office. His brother did not warm up to people easily. He had poor interpersonal skills. However the idea was to put his brother in an environment that would force him to work. If he was left in an office on his own, he would not work.

Fady and Emily walked down the hall and took a left turn. There was a door right at the end. Emily was not too familiar with that part of the building. Fady opened the door and gestured for Emily to walk in first. She glared around the room as she walked in. There was a long table in the middle of the room and leather chairs around it. There were two laptops on the table. The room had large windows with no blinds or curtains. Emily liked that because it allowed the sun to shine into the room. There was also a cute seating area with a loveseat sofa and two armchairs. There was a coffee table in front of the sofas.

"It's nice," Emily said to Fady.

"I am glad that it is to your liking," he replied.

"How come the time scale is so short for the project?" Emily spat out. She was so curious. She had to ask.

"It's a customer's requirement and also my brother is in a bit of bind. He has to be successful on this project."

Emily was not satisfied with the answer but she could not further interrogate him. She just nodded. The word "bind" resonated in her head. What kind of bind was Basil in? It only made her more curious.

Chapter 4

After Fady had left, Emily returned to her office to collect her bag. She also picked up a few items that she thought she would need and then headed back to the office that Fady had chosen for her and Basil. The office was nice, it was beautiful and comfortable. When she re-entered the room, she noticed that there was a small fridge. She opened it and found some drinks and snacks. She shut the door and went to sit at the table. Emily flipped open one of the brand-new looking laptops that sat on the table and was glad to see that the software she used to analyze land had already been installed.

Almost an hour and a half later, Basil finally arrived. He walked into the room dressed in black trousers and a navy blue shirt. Emily looked up from the laptop at him. He looked at Emily with his eyebrows crossed. "Good morning," she greeted him. He turned on his heel and walked back out of the room. He headed to his brother's office.

Basil opened the door to Fady's office and let himself in. Fady was sitting at his desk. He looked up when Basil walked in. "You forgot to mention one important thing to me when you told me about my office," Basil said, still standing in the doorway. Fady gave Basil a questioning look. He put his pen down and leaned back in his seat.

"What did I forget to mention?" Fady asked.

"That I am to share the office."

A small smile appeared on Fady's face. He knew that his brother was not going to like the idea. It did not shock him that his brother had stormed into his office to discuss the matter. "Well, the two of you are going to be working together. It makes sense to share an office," said Fady.

"No, it does not. We can work from separate offices." Basil had never had to share anything with anyone. The only time he was in a room with someone else, it was either a servant serving him, or a member of his family or a female companion. Other than that, there was no reason for him to sit in the same room with a mere person.

"The two of you need to come up with a plan and discuss everything. You cannot be communicating through secretaries," said Fady. Basil stared at him with a blank facial expression.

"So you are telling me that I have to share an office, with her, every day, for three months?"

"Basil, stop overreacting and go do your work."

"This is a terrible idea, I am telling you."

Fady laughed a little. He understood that his brother had never worked or had to get along with people he did not know. "All you have to do is be cordial and professional," he said. Basil grunted and turned on his heel. He headed out of Fady's office and returned to the office that he was sharing with Emily.

When he walked back into the room, Emily was still sitting at the table looking at her laptop. She looked at him when he walked back in. He pulled out a chair and sat down. He flipped the laptop open and tapped a key. It was just around 11:30 a.m., and he could not wait to get the day over and done with.

Emily felt awkward. She did not know why he had walked out of the office after he first came in. He had not even replied to her when she greeted him. She did not know whether to greet him again or not. She took a deep breath and started speaking.

"Given the time we have, I do not think we should do coring," Emily began. Every time she had tried to be polite to Basil, he had not returned her politeness. So this time she just went straight to the point.

"Why not?" Basil asked without looking up from his laptop. At least this time it was not his phone that he was holding onto.

"Takes long and it's too expensive."

"What then?"

"Well logging," she said. Both well logging and coring were methods of analyzing rock and earth samples. The petrophysicists then studied the data obtained from the analysis and formed their conclusions on whether there was fuel or not, the quantity of the fuel, and how to proceed with the drilling.

"Okay," Basil replied.

"Shall I explain well logging to you?" Emily asked. She thought maybe he was not aware of the methods, since he was not saying much.

"I know what well logging is." Basil finally looked up.

"It's just that you are not saying much." Emily was losing her patience with him.

"Do I need to talk to you? I just need to do my work."

"Yes, you do need to talk to me. We have to work together, we cannot just work separately and then compare notes later."

"It works for me."

"We have no time to spare," said Emily.

"Three months is plenty," said Basil lazily.

"It is just enough time if we put all our effort in." Emily sighed. "Prince Fady says that you're in a bit of a bind," she added.

"It is none of your business," Basil replied.

"It is clear to me that you do not want to work with me but we have no choice in the matter. So we should just get on with it," Emily said. She tried to ignore his rudeness. He probably felt that he could get away with it just because he was a prince.

Basil sighed. "We should," he said. In the end it was him who was going to lose out if the project was not successful. Emily nodded. Finally, something they both agreed on.

They discussed well logging in more detail. They needed to start that very day. Everything had to be done fast. Emily called the geology department and asked them to start the well logging that day. They talked some more about the project. Emily did most of the talking, of course.

She was surprised, however, whenever Basil spoke. He did not talk much but he was quite smart. He came up with very good points. When it was four in the afternoon, Basil left first. Emily buried her head in her hands. She was glad that they were no longer together. He was just frustrating. He had come late and now he had left early. He was a piece of work. She stayed behind and did some work until it was six. She tidied up the office and then headed home.

Chapter 5

Emily rushed towards the elevator the next morning when she arrived at work. Fady held the doors open for her. She leaped into the elevator and smiled at him. "Thank you," she said. He nodded in response. Emily stood next to him quietly.

"How was your first day working with my brother?" Fady asked Emily. He knew his brother very well. Basil was like a wrecking ball in every woman's life. If he was not sleeping with her, then he was very unkind and diabolic towards her. If he was sleeping with a woman, he lost interest quickly and tossed her aside. He made women feel worthless and unwanted. That was his nature. He was a prince that cared for no one except himself.

"It was fine," Emily replied.

"I doubt it." Fady had a small smile on his face. The lift doors opened and the two of them walked out. The receptionist, Rachel, stood up and greeted Fady. He gave her a nod as he and Emily walked past her.

"Honestly, it was fine."

Fady looked down at Emily as they were walking. He did not believe her at all. Emily could feel his gaze. She turned to look at him and saw him looking at her with his eyebrow raised. "It was fine," Fady repeated sarcastically. Emily looked away and sighed.

"He is not easy to work with," she blurted out. She was sure that it was not the right move to talk about Basil to his brother but Fady was trying to drag it out of her. He knew that Emily and Basil were not getting along.

"Yes, that is true, you will just have to bear with him. If it gets too hard, come find me."

"It will be okay." She hoped that it was going to be okay because she was a Southern girl and Southern girls did not take crap from anyone. She did not want to lose it on her boss's brother but if he kept up with his rudeness, she would have to speak her mind.

"It will get hard, come find me then." Fady quickened his pace and took a left turn, towards his office.

Instead of feeling good that Fady was willing to come to her aid if working with Basil was too hard, Emily was worrying that it was going to get hard. She headed to her office. Just as she was about to walk in, she remembered that she was to be working in a different office now. She frowned and turned around. She headed to the office she was sharing with Basil. When she walked into the empty room, she was not surprised to see he was not there.

She put her bag down. Fortunately there was a coffee machine in the room. There was almost everything she needed in the new office. She walked towards the machine and started making herself some coffee. She heard the door open. She turned and saw Basil walking in. She raised her eyebrows in surprise. He was actually on time.

"What is wrong with you?" he asked her. She frowned.

"Good morning to you too," she replied sardonically and looked away. It was too early in the day to deal with his attitude. He did not respond to her. He just pulled out a chair and sat down instead. "Coffee?" she asked him.

"One and a half teaspoon of coffee, one quarter of almond milk and three quarters water and one teaspoon of brown sugar," said Basil. Emily stared at him with a blank facial expression.

"Rather specific," she said.

"I like my things a certain way."

"I see."

"Make sure to wash the cup first."

Emily raised her eyebrow. Did Basil think that she was his maid or something? She did not answer him and made his coffee the same way she made hers. Basil seemed like a fussy man. She was not going to make the coffee the way he had asked. She walked over to the table with two white mugs in her hand. She placed a mug right in front of Basil. He looked up from his phone and studied the coffee for a second before he sipped it.

"This is not how I drink it," Basil said. He could immediately taste the difference. He always drank coffee the same way. He could taste any minor change.

"That is how you will drink it today," Emily said as she sat down and sipped her coffee. She placed the mug down and flipped the laptop open. Basil put the coffee down as if it were something disgusting.

"I will not drink it."

"Suit yourself." Emily took another sip of her coffee. That was the last time she was ever making him coffee. She knew he was not going to get up to make himself another cup. She looked at him from the corner of her eye. He was on his phone and not drinking his coffee. "What do you do in Al-Bisha?" she asked him.

"Why do you want to know?"

"You are always on your phone. Either you have a business or many female companions."

Basil looked up from his phone and looked at her. He had his eyebrows raised. He did not say anything to her. Instead he studied her. She was wearing a white sleeveless turtleneck top and a black high-waisted skirt. Her hair was tied up in a high bun. She was average looking.

"What?" Emily asked him. His stare was making her feel uncomfortable. He had just stared at her and not said anything.

Basil did not respond immediately. Emily could feel his cold gaze piercing through her. "Nothing," he finally said and looked down at his phone. Emily looked at her laptop. His cold stare made her a little uncomfortable. She just hoped that he did not notice.

A little later in the day, Rachel walked in the room with a folder for Emily. The folder had some important information regarding a previous project. She bowed her head to Basil and smiled. "Good afternoon, your highness," she greeted him but he did not answer. He did not even look up. He acted as though he had not heard her. Emily creased her eyebrows.

"Hi, Rachel," Emily greeted her.

"Hello, Emily," she replied. She approached her and gave her the folder.

"Thanks, have there been any messages from the geology department?"

"No, nothing yet. I will let you know as soon as I hear something."

"Sure."

Rachel bowed to Basil before she left. He barely flinched. Emily had seen the entire thing. She felt bad for Rachel. Basil was just pompous and Rachel did not deserve that.

"You could have answered her," Emily said.

"Why?" Basil asked.

"Because it is polite."

Basil grunted in response. Rachel was just like a palace maid. There was no need for him to answer to her. He did not care what Emily thought of his actions. He certainly did not care for her opinion. He looked at his wrist, it was around three already. He had been there since morning. He closed his laptop.

"Where are you going?" Emily asked him. Basil shrugged. He was certainly not going to answer her question. It was none of her business. He stood up and walked out of the room. Emily growled. She was starting to see what Fady was talking about. His brother was difficult. *Just approximately 87 days left to the end of the project,* Emily thought to herself.

Chapter 6

Emily welcomed the weekend with a big smile. She was glad that she was not going to be dealing with Prince Basil for the next two days. She just wanted to stay home and relax. However that plan was quickly crushed. Her grandmother came over to her house and forced Emily to accompany her to the country club.

"I really do not want to go," Emily complained to her grandmother.

"Just get dressed quickly," her grandmother replied. Emily reluctantly went to her room to get dressed. She knew that if she tried to deny her grandmother's request, she could only lose. Her grandmother would not leave her alone so easily. She would probably emotionally blackmail Emily by saying that she was old and would die soon, so it would be wise for Emily to spend every chance she got with her. After Emily had finished getting ready, she returned downstairs and headed out of the house with her grandmother. They left in Emily's car. The country club was only a 10-minute drive away.

When they arrived, Emily's grandmother pulled out her parking pass and slapped it on the dashboard. They both got out of the car and headed inside. Even though the club was for members only, they were allowed a plus-one on weekends. So Emily was allowed to come with her grandmother. The country club was great for a lot of activities such as horseback riding, swimming, golf, gymnasium, and tennis.

"Why did you bring me here?" Emily asked her grandmother.

"I think there will be more bachelors by the stables," she replied. Emily whipped her head in her grandmother's direction and looked at her.

"You have got to be kidding me, Nana."

"What?"

"Bachelors?"

"You cannot stay single forever. I want to see my great-grandchildren before I die."

Emily rolled her eyes. She had been tricked once again. The last time her grandmother had tricked her into going on a cruise with her. It turned out that it was a singles cruise. Her grandmother took her hand and led her towards the horse stables. There weren't many people by the stables, just a few men.

"So what is your plan now, Nana?" Emily asked. She wished that she could just run off and go back home but she could not leave her grandmother there.

"Sit by the track," she replied. Emily reluctantly followed her grandmother to the track, where some men were riding. A lady was already standing by the fence. She had long jet-black hair, olive skin, and jet-black eyebrows. She was wearing a boat-neck blue dress that hugged her breasts and then flared. She had a white Michael Kors clutch bag. A man riding on a horse stopped in front of her and got off the horse. Emily was hardly paying attention.

"You ride well," the woman said to him. She had an accent.

"I do," the man replied. Emily recognized his voice. She turned and saw that it was Basil. She immediately felt awkward. He turned his head and locked eyes with Emily. He raised his eyebrows slightly. "What are you doing here?" he asked her.

"I could ask you the same thing," she replied.

"I am a member here and I do not think you are one."

"Why would I not be one?" Emily frowned. Just what was he suggesting? Sure, country clubs were for rich people and she was not rich but he knew nothing about her life. How dare he insinuate?

Basil scanned her from head to toe before he replied. "For one, your attire is incorrect," he said. Emily was wearing white trousers and a white T-shirt. She frowned at him. This was the second time he had said something about her dress sense.

"It is none of your business how I dress," Emily replied. Her grandmother was standing next to her watching the squabble between her granddaughter and the unfamiliar man unfold.

"Who is she?" the lady in the blue dress asked Basil.

"Had you been a member, you would dress differently," Basil said to Emily, and ignored the lady in the blue dress. Emily rolled her eyes.

"It's my day off, I do not have to speak to you," she said. She looked at her grandmother. "Nana, let's go," she said to her.

"Who is he?" Emily's grandmother asked.

"Someone I have the unfortunate pleasure of working with," she replied.

"It is I who is unfortunate," Basil said.

"You work together?" the lady in the blue dress asked.

"Wait for me in the car," he said to her. She nodded and walked off. Emily raised her eyebrows.

"One of your female lovers?" Emily asked.

"You have quite an interest in my private affairs," Basil said and crossed his arms over his chest.

"I do not."

"You do."

"Like I said, it is my day off and I do not have to speak to you," Emily said and walked off. Her grandmother followed her. Emily was not sure where she was going but she just wanted to get away from Basil. Seeing him had just spoiled her day. She walked past the stables and into the main building of the club. She walked straight down the hall and took a right a turn. She finally stopped when she reached a spot that looked like a reception area.

"Who is he?" her grandmother asked her once they had stopped walking. She had been following her granddaughter and watched her practically running away from the man she was speaking to. "Don't worry, he is not chasing you," she joked.

"He is Prince Basil," Emily replied.

"He is a prince?" Her nana's eyes widened and a small smile appeared on her face.

"Yes, Nana. Can we go home?"

"We just got here," said her grandmother. "There was something between you and him."

"Yes, mutual detestation," said Emily.

Her grandmother laughed. "The opposite," she said. She walked towards the sofas that were in the corner of the room. Emily followed her with a frown on her face.

"What opposite?" she asked her grandmother as she sat in front of her.

"I have been on this earth longer than you have. I can see things you cannot."

"Like what?"

"There is chemistry between you and the prince."

Emily stared at her grandmother with a frown on her face. It seemed as though her nana did not know what she was talking about. Emily and Basil did not get along. Whenever they were with one another, they seemed to be fighting about something. How could there possibly be chemistry between them?

"Yes, there is chemistry," Emily said sarcastically.

"You argue with passion."

"Okay, lady. I am done talking about *him*. Can we please go home?"

"No, I saved all my pennies to get this country club membership. So we are going to enjoy this place, young lady."

Emily moaned. She never had wanted to come to the country club in the first place. Now she really wanted to leave because of Basil. She did not want to risk running into him again. She crossed her fingers and hoped that was not the case. Emily and her grandmother stood up and decided to go have some food.

"He is handsome though," said Nana.

"Oh, Nana, it seems you need glasses already," Emily replied.

"It seems you need them if you do not think that young prince is handsome."

Emily laughed. "He is average, nothing special," she said. Her nana shook her head.

"Instead of arguing with him, you should befriend him. He's a prince," she said.

"A very rude one."

"He did have a point."

"What point?"

"You could dress a little better."

Emily rolled her eyes. Her nana and her aunt always told her that her dress sense was average but average did not turn heads. She needed to dress in a sexy but classy way, so that she turned heads and caught the attention of the bachelors.

Chapter 7

"You are here early," Fady said to Basil as he walked into his office.

"I am, but she isn't," Basil said, referring to Emily. She had not arrived in the office yet.

"How it is working with her?"

"It is obviously not great," said Basil. Fady laughed a little and shook his head. "As if that is not enough, I had to see her at the country club," he added. Fady raised his eyebrows.

"She is a member?"

"I doubt it."

"So mother called me. The baby is not yours."

"Of course it is not mine," Basil replied. One of his former female lovers had come to the palace a month ago claiming that she was carrying his child. Basil had rejected her and said that the baby wasn't his.

"I just cannot believe that you were not even willing to take responsibility if it was your child," said Fady. Basil just shrugged his shoulders. He was not ready to be a father yet.

"Well, that does not matter now since she lied."

"Brother, these antics of yours need to end. You have to start taking responsibility and mature."

Basil put his phone down on the table and looked at Fady. "I am living just fine," he said.

"Isn't that why you are in this current predicament?" Fady asked, referring to the fact that Basil's title was on the line. Just then, Emily walked into the room.

"Well, it is not my fault that he does not approve my way of life. I was not destined to work in the oil business and I do not want to be forced," said Basil.

"Well, you have to do something."

Emily immediately felt awkward. She had no idea what she had just walked into. "Shall I leave?" she asked Fady. She was pretty sure that she was not meant to be hearing that conversation.

"No, you need to hear this actually," Fady said to her.

"Are you sure?"

"The reason why this project is so important is because if it is not successful, our father the king will strip Basil's title as prince."

Emily's eye flew open. What had she just heard? And why had she heard it?

"That is none of her business," Basil said. He did not exactly want Emily getting involved in his life or even knowing about him.

"She needs to know. Maybe the two of you will be a little bit motivated," Fady replied.

"Why? What happened for such a drastic decision?" Emily asked. She was suddenly more intrigued by Basil now. Just what was he all about?

"That is none of your business," Basil said to her. Fady tapped her shoulder and walked out of the room. Emily felt even more curious. They had just revealed something so big to her and then not told her the details. She hated being told half the story. She walked over to her seat and placed her bag on the table. She took off her blazer. She then went to make herself some coffee. While she was waiting for it to be done, she turned and looked at Basil.

"Given the reason why we are doing this project together and in such a short time span, shouldn't you be a bit more hard-working?" she asked. She had to say it, he was slacking.

"More hard-working?" Basil asked.

"You always leave early and when you are here, you are on your phone."

"You pay attention to my every move."

Emily rolled her eyes and poured herself the coffee. "Please do not be conceited," she said.

"Stay out of my business," he warned. Emily walked over to her seat with her coffee. "You are not making me coffee?" he asked. Emily let out a laugh.

"No, last time I made you coffee, you were ungrateful." She took a sip of her coffee and smiled as she swallowed. It tasted heavenly.

"So you expect me to make it myself?"

"Precisely."

Basil looked at her as if she were mad. There was no way he was going to get up and make himself coffee. Fortunately for him, Rachel walked in. Just like the last time she had come in the office, she greeted Basil with a bow and a smile.

"Make me a cup of coffee," he said to her.

"Yes, your highness. How do you like it?" she replied. He gave her the same instructions he had told Emily. Rachel nodded and left the room. Emily was staring at Basil. She shook her head.

"You are shameless," she said to him.

"Excuse me?" Basil replied.

"You ignored the girl last time and now you just order her around."

"She works for my family company. I can do that if I want to." Basil had a smirk on his face. Emily just looked away. He was just too arrogant and conceited. Moments later, Rachel returned to the office with a folder in her hand and a cup of coffee for Basil. He did not even thank her when she gave it to him. She handed Emily the folder.

"Results from the geology department," she said.

"Thank you," Emily replied. Rachel bowed to Basil before she left. Emily opened the folder and pulled out the results of the well logging. She moved closer to Basil so that they could discuss the results. He looked up from his phone and looked at Emily.

"Why are you moving closer to me?" he asked her.

"To discuss the results," she said and passed him the papers with the graphs and data.

"Are you certain that it is not an excuse for you to be near me?"

Emily narrowed her gaze at him. "Are you serious right now?" she said. He stared at her and said nothing. He looked serious. "Just look at the results," she said to him. She did not want to have another staring contest with him. It was just too intense.

"Do I make you uncomfortable?" he asked her.

"What are you talking about now?"

"When I am looking at you, I can see you slowly unraveling."

"You are conceited," Emily said. She did not unravel! Yes, he made her feel uncomfortable but not unravel. He picked up a sheet of results without taking his eyes off her face. He smirked and then looked down at the paper. It took him seconds to make sense of the results. It surprised Emily because he had not been that vocal on the project and she still did not understand what his role was in the whole thing.

"The methane in this field is promising," he said.

"You can interpret well logs?" Emily asked him

"Of course I can."

"You are smarter than you look."

Basil raised an eyebrow. "What is that supposed to mean?" he asked.

"Well, you have not been working, you barely say anything, you act like you do not care."

"So you assumed."

Emily shrugged her shoulders and leaned forward. When she leaned forward, she got a whiff of Basil's scent. He smelled very pleasantly. She found herself noticing his strong jaw. His body was just as strong.

Basil moved closer to Emily. "Why are you studying me?" he asked her. His voice had gone deeper. Emily widened her eyes.

"I was not," she lied. She had not done so intentionally. It just sort of happened. Basil grabbed her chin with index finger and thumb. His gaze was so intense, Emily felt her stomach knot up. She stared back at him wide-eyed. She wondered why he was holding her like that and staring at her face. She hated how much he was affecting her in that moment. She pressed her knees together to stop them from knocking.

"Here is a closer look," he said.

"Let me go," she said.

"You feel nervous."

"I don't."

"I make you uncomfortable."

"You don't."

"Really?" he asked and started moving closer to Emily's face.

Chapter 8

Basil moved closer to Emily's face until their noses were almost touching. Emily's eyes widened. She did not know what he was doing or why he was doing it. She started feeling very nervous and uncomfortable. She pressed her knees together even harder. She could smell him and he smelled really good. She felt her face heating up. Emily pushed him away. "What are you doing?" she asked him and looked away. Basil laughed a little.

"See," he said.

"See what?"

"I make you uncomfortable." Basil leaned back in his chair. He was practically gloating like he had proved something. Emily was avoiding eye contact with him. She was full of mixed emotions. She was nervous about him being so close to her. She had also found herself noticing his full lips and his strong jaw.

"No, you do not," Emily protested.

"Yes, I do."

"Let's just focus on our work."

"Yes, you need to focus on the work, not on me."

Emily rolled her eyes. He was so conceited. Emily picked up her laptop and returned to her seat at the edge of the table. She could not believe what had just happened. She cleared her throat and just focused on her laptop.

***

Finally the drilling had begun. So far the plan had been moving along fine. Fady called Emily and Basil into his office for a meeting. The two sat opposite Fady at his desk. There was enough distance between them to fit another chair. Their disdain for each other was obvious. Fady thought they would have at least warmed up to each other after working together for almost two weeks now. However that did not seem to be the case.

Fady asked for an update on the methane project. Emily started telling him about the progress they had made so far. Basil was just sitting back in his chair with his phone in his hand. It was no surprise to Fady. His younger brother had always showed no interest in the family business.

"Basil, is this the case?" Fady asked him.

"Yes," he said without looking up from his phone. Emily frowned. *What was the point of asking Basil anything?* she thought to herself. He hadn't been mentally present most of the time. She had done most of the work. Fair enough, she had seen him interpret the results but that was about the only work he had done. It was surprising to her that he was that smart. She wondered why though.

"I am glad things are working out," said Fady. "Well, the reason that I called you in is because I need to inform you on an upcoming meeting with Magenta Oils. They have requested some methane samples," he added. Basil frowned.

"So you need us to take the samples to the meeting?" Emily asked. Fady nodded as he leaned back into his chair. "When is the meeting?" Emily asked.

"In a week's time. Will you be ready?" Fady asked.

"Yes, we will."

"Good." Fady nodded.

"If there is nothing else, I will return to my work now," said Emily. Fady nodded, he had nothing more to say to her. Emily got up and left the office. Fady turned his attention to Basil.

"You will not be returning to your work either?" Fady asked Basil, who was still sitting comfortably in his seat.

"Not at this moment," he replied truthfully.

"How is it working with Emily?"

Basil grunted before he responded. First off, *working* was just not great. He did not like having to come into work every day. He liked to do things on his own accord. Second, working with someone he was not fond of was even worse. Basil frowned as he remembered himself teasing her. He had intentionally moved closer to her as if he was going to kiss her, only to tease her. He felt strangely afterwards. He had not anticipated feeling anything. It bothered him.

"It is what it is," Basil finally replied.

"By now, I would have expected you to have warmed up to her."

"I have not done anything to her. I am civil towards her. That is enough."

"You need to call mother," said Fady. Basil slid in his phone in his pocket.

"Why?" he asked his brother. He had an awful feeling that he knew what it was about. Fady laughed softly.

"Because she wants to speak to you," Fady answered Basil. "You realize that you cannot dodge marriage forever, right?"

"I am not interested in the brides she has in mind for me, nor am I interested in the idea of marriage at the moment," said Basil. He had never pictured himself as a husband. To him marriage was being tied down to one woman for the rest of his life. That was not appealing to him. He got bored rather easily. No one woman could keep him interested for longer than two weeks. The longest he had ever been with the same woman was a month.

"She did well with choosing my wife," said Fady. Their mother had chosen his wife for him. Fortunately, they liked each other.

"Well, that is great for you but I do not wish to be married."

"You will have to someday."

Basil sighed. "Just not today," he said.

"You know mother is relentless. This matter will not die down easily," said Fady.

"I know, that is why I will avoid her for as long as I can." Basil rose to his feet.

"So you have decided to get back to your work now?" Fady said jokingly.

"What choice do I have?" he replied as he slid his hands into his pockets. He stalked out the exit and headed to the office he shared with Emily.

Chapter 9

"No, you can't leave!" Emily said to Basil as she blocked the door with her body. There were only a few days left before their meeting with Magenta Oils and she wanted to prepare with Basil but as always he wanted to leave early. They needed to be in sync, know what they were going to talk about at the meeting. Emily had had enough of Basil not caring. He was too relaxed. She figured that she would do everything in her power to stop him from leaving and at that moment, it meant blocking the exit.

"And why not?" Basil asked Emily.

"Because we have to prepare for the meeting."

"What is there to prepare? We are going to meet with the company and hand them methane samples. It's not rocket science."

Emily rolled her eyes. Basil was really testing her patience. He was the worst person to work with. He had basically done nothing. She wished she could stop working with him but it was not an option.

"Would you get out of the way?" Basil asked her.

"No. You can't leave, not yet," Emily replied with her hands on her hips. Basil was a little bit amused by her. Did she think that she could stop him from doing whatever he wanted? She was half his size. He moved closer to her and looked down at her.

Emily felt a little intimidated by his physique. He was much taller than her and quite muscular. He towered over her and he looked at her with a blank gaze. She could not imagine what he was thinking and it made her nervous. All of a sudden he grabbed her by the waist and picked her up. "What are you doing?" Emily cried out.

"Moving you out of the way, since you refused to get out of the way," he replied. He turned around, holding her up in the air, and then he put her down. "You are very heavy," he teased. She did not weigh much to him. He lifted weights heavier than her in the gym.

"I did not ask you to pick me up." Emily frowned and pushed him away.

"You are so aggressive."

"And you are so annoying." Emily pushed him again. It was pointless because it made no impact. Basil barely moved an inch, which frustrated her even more. He held the back of her neck and pulled her face closer to his. He pressed his lips firmly against hers. Emily protested by attempting to push him away, which did not work. Basil only kissed her even more.

Emily hit his chest softly before she gave up and just kissed him back. He deepened the kiss by allowing his tongue inside of her mouth. He kissed her so gently and passionately, as if he was exploring her mouth.

Realization sunk in and he broke off this kiss. *This was Emily,* for goodness' sake, he thought to himself. It was the same woman who spoke rudely to him and constantly nagged him about the damned project. She was annoying and she was definitely not his type. However her lips had been so tempting, and she had an alluring scent. Basil turned on his heel and left the room.

Emily was left feeling rather confused. She could not figure out why Basil had just kissed her. Emily touched her lips, where his lips had been. Although the kiss had happened quickly, it had affected her greatly. Just that one kiss had set her body on fire. No one had ever kissed her like that. Her hands were still shaking. But how could that be? She disliked him, he was arrogant, lazy, and rude. She should not have enjoyed the kiss, she shouldn't have even allowed him to kiss her. Emily just sighed and sat down at the table.

***

Emily was attempting to have a peaceful dinner with her family but it was impossible since her mother and grandmother were always arguing. Her aunt tried to be the peacemaker but it never helped. Emily and her brothers were wise to stay out of it. All of a sudden Emily's grandmother turned her attention to Emily.

"How is that handsome young man?" she asked her. Emily crossed her eyebrows.

"What man?" Emily asked.

"The handsome prince we met at the country club."

Emily narrowed her gaze at her grandmother. She did not want to discuss Basil. Talking about him would only remind her of the last time she saw him, when he kissed her. Thinking about it still made her nervous and shy.

"Who is this guy who is making you turn red?" Sandy, Emily's aunt, asked her.

"What? No, I am not turning red!" Emily protested.

"You are," said her brother Jake.

"Shut up."

Emily's grandmother started laughing at how defensive Emily was. "But what is wrong with him?" she asked Emily.

"He's just so arrogant and lazy. I would rather not work with him. I just want to enjoy my food, can we not speak about him?"

"She seems like she hates the man," said James, her other brother.

"Hate is the opposite of love. They're both strong emotions to feel," said her grandmother.

"I do not hate him," Emily said as she stood up with her plate. There was no point in eating. Her family would not allow her to eat. First it was because of her grandmother and mother fighting, now it was all of them teasing her about Basil.

"Well, you seem like you really dislike him," said Sandy.

"You have not finished your food," said Tina, Emily's mother.

"I am full. I am going home to prepare for my meeting tomorrow!" Emily replied. She was grateful that this family Sunday lunch was not being held at her house. They normally did it at her grandmother's house. If they were in Emily's house, she would have not been able to leave. She would have had to stay until everyone left.

"No you are not leaving, young lady. This is family time!"

"But, Mom, I have a very important meeting." Emily didn't have one but she was running away from talking about Basil. When her family started speaking about a certain topic, they did not give up. They would keep on talking about it until they reached the bottom of the matter.

"She is old enough to do what she wants. Let her go," said her grandmother. Emily rolled her eyes. That was the beginning of yet another disagreement between her mother and grandmother. Her grandmother was her mother's mother-in-law. They had never gotten along from day one. Now that Emily's father was not in the picture, after her parents' divorce, they no longer pretended to like each other.

Chapter 10

Emily arrived at the Tadros refinery where the company refined their oils. She and Basil were coming separately. The businessmen from Magenta Oils were coming to meet with Emily and Basil at the refinery and to collect the methane samples. It was also an opportunity for them to see where the methane was going to get converted into liquid and then packaged for transport.

As Emily waited, she wondered where Basil was. He was not late yet but he was unpredictable. Emily was worried that he might show up late as he always did at the office. He had just showed how uninterested he was. She could not help but expect the worst. Emily just took a deep breath and kept on waiting. She had no choice but to wait.

Basil finally showed up right on time. His car parked just next to hers. Emily sighed with relief and got out of the car. She saw the businessmen from Magenta Oils arriving also.

"Where the heck were you?" Emily said to Basil as soon as he got out of the car. If Basil had been just a minute later, he would have arrived later than the Magenta Oils people and that would not have looked good. He looked at her with a cold gaze as always.

"I am here, aren't I?" he asked her. Emily was not surprised. He did not even care.

"Let's just go now." She wanted to yell at him for his laziness and lack of motivation. However, this was not the time for it. They had a meeting to conduct. Afterwards, she was definitely going to speak her mind. She could not hold it any longer.

Basil and Emily walked towards the people from Magenta Oils together. Emily smiled at them when they approached, as if she was not annoyed because of Basil.

"Good morning, I am Emily Gibson," she introduced herself. "And this Basil Tadros," she added.

Basil was shocked that Emily had introduced him as just Basil Tadros. Was she out of her mind? He was a prince and had to be referred to as one at all times. It was so disrespectful of her. Back in his home country, everyone referred to him by his rightful title. As much as Basil wanted to correct her, he kept a poker face on. It was a business meeting.

"Good morning, Miss Gibson," one man said and shook her hand. He introduced himself as Mr. Johns. He also shook Basil's hand. He then introduced the other two men to Emily and Basil. The three of them had met with Fady previously to discuss the business deal between Magenta Oils and the Tadros Oil Company.

"How is your father?" Mr. Johns asked Basil. One of the things that had made Magenta Oils people want to work with them was the Tadros name. They were well-known in the oil industry. Tadros Oil Company was quite successful.

"The sheikh is well," Basil replied.

"We know of his work when he first started the business. His legacy is quite impressive."

"I assure you that Fady and I follow his footsteps."

Emily completely disagreed. She did not know the sheikh but she knew Basil. And he had a poor work ethic.

"I hope so." Mr. Johns smiled.

"If you sign the contract with us, we will provide the methane at a good price. We will convert the methane into liquid at 10% discount, and if you need our technicians to change it back to gas, that will be free of charge," he said. Mr. Johns nodded and laughed. He was definitely interested and impressed by what Basil was saying.

"Sweetening the deal just like your father," he said. He looked impressed. Emily was surprised. Basil was actually speaking sense. He was doing well. She had not expected that from him.

Basil and Mr. Johns kept on talking. The other men listened and spoke a few words. They too seemed impressed by Basil. When they had finished touring the refinery, they returned to the entrance where Emily and Basil bid them farewell. Their methane samples had already been loaded into the truck. Emily waited for them to leave before she turned to Basil.

"Just what is wrong with you?" she asked him. He looked at her with his eyebrow raised.

"What now?" he asked her.

"You should have come a bit earlier, and not at the same time as the clients. You just turn up late like it is okay."

"That again." Basil narrowed his gaze at her.

"Yes, that. You are seriously playing around and it has got to end." Emily had kept quiet all along because he was her boss's younger brother. However she could not tolerate it any longer.

"Get off my case. I came, I delivered–" Before he could finish speaking, Emily cut him off.

"Yes, you delivered, surprisingly. It shows you are capable which makes things worse. It means that you are just lazy," she said.

Basil slid his hands in his pockets and just looked at her. Since she was so feisty and was going to cut him off, there was no point in speaking. He just thought to let her continue speaking until she was done.

"This is an important project, for the company and for you. I believe you should at least put some effort in," she added. So many thoughts were rushing through her mind. She wanted to yell at him for his lack of caring and she wanted to praise him for doing well with Magenta Oils.

"Are you finished?" he asked her.

"You are so rude," she said with her hands on her hips.

"I believe you are the one who verbally attacked me first."

"With good reason."

"You need to remember who I am," he said. Emily crossed her arms over her chest. "You will address me as your highness or Prince Basil," he continued. Emily burst out laughing.

"You are full of yourself," she said. There was no way she was going to refer to him as your highness.

"Have your opinions, I do not care. I am still a prince and you need to acknowledge that."

"Have you ever worked in the methane business or do you have relevant education?" Emily asked. She had been curious as to how he had so much knowledge regarding the methane business.

"What does that have to do with anything?" he asked with a frown on his face.

"Just curious." That she was and also she did not want speak about his title. She was never going to address him the way he wanted her to.

"I should not have to explain myself to you," he said and started walking off. Emily walked with him.

"So it's just by chance." Emily sighed. Basil stopped walking and looked at her. Normally he did not justify himself to anyone but he felt the need to with Emily.

"Not that it's any of your business but I have a PhD in petroleum engineering," he said to her. Emily raised her eyebrows. She did not expect that at all. Maybe a degree but not a PhD. It was quite impressive. She had never been so impressed by him. He was appearing more and more attractive in her eyes. Yes, she had noticed that he was handsome but did not pay attention to it because of his rudeness. However right now, finding out that he was intelligent and seeing his potential, and having him staring at her, made him very attractive in her eyes.

Basil started remembering the kiss they had shared. He had enjoyed it more than he had expected. Standing there and staring at her made him want to kiss her again. She was so short and fit in his arms perfectly. Her hourglass figure was enticing. He crossed his eyebrows and walked off. He could not trust himself not to kiss her again. The best thing was to walk away.

Emily exhaled with relief when Basil turned to walk away. The way he had been looking at her had made her feel nervous. She could not figure out what he was thinking. It was the same look he had given her before he kissed her the last time, but he was not possibly going to kiss her again. Part of her wanted him to kiss her again. She could not understand what she was feeling. She couldn't possibly be attracted to Basil, that cold and rude man. There was no way. She shook the thoughts away and headed to her car.

Chapter 11

It had been two days since Emily had seen Basil. She had last seen him on Monday at the refinery. Even after that speech she had given him, he still was not motivated to work. It truly annoyed her. She was no longer bothered about him. The hard work had been done really. Now they just had to wait to hear back from Magenta Oils, and know whether they had approved of the sample. Emily had been working on her other projects that had taken a back seat because of the methane project.

She got up from the desk and went to make herself a cup of coffee. As she was waiting for it to brew, she heard the door open and then someone speaking to her. "Make a cup for me too," the person said. She recognized the voice instantly. She did not even bother to turn around.

"So you decided to show up," she said without turning around.

"There is nothing to do anyway," Basil replied. Emily heard him pull out a chair.

"That is not the point."

"I want mine a little strong today."

"Your what?" Emily asked as she poured herself some coffee. She poured in some milk and two teaspoons of sugar.

"My coffee," he replied. Emily laughed. She turned around and walked back to her seat.

"You are funny. I have never made you any coffee, what makes you think that I will do so today?" She took a sip of her coffee, looking at him. She intentionally teased him with her coffee.

"You are so stingy," he said to her. Emily laughed as she sat down.

"You need to learn how to ask politely."

Basil grunted as he got up. He went to the coffee machine. He grunted again when he realized that she had not made much coffee. There was a just a little bit of coffee left, it was not even enough to make a cup. He pulled out the coffee beans.

"Are my eyes deceiving me?" Emily asked. She could not believe that Basil was actually about to make himself coffee.

"Well you refused, didn't you?"

"Hold on, let me get out my phone and take a picture of this!" Emily said jokingly.

"This would have never happened in the palace."

"Well, we aren't in the palace."

Basil grunted. "No need to remind me," he said.

"You miss it?" Emily asked him as he examined the coffee machine, wondering where to put the coffee beans.

"Of course I do. It's my home," he replied. Emily started laughing. "What is so funny?" he asked her. She put her coffee mug down and stood up. She walked over to him.

"The fact that you cannot make coffee," she replied. She took coffee beans from him and put in them in the correct section of the coffee machine.

"Well, would it have been easier if you had made it for me from the start," he said.

"I did not know you would be this useless at making coffee."

"Women." He sighed. "You are all so difficult."

Emily switched on the machine. She crossed her arms over her chest and looked at him. "There is a woman making life difficult?" she asked him. He raised his eyebrows before he responded.

"Look how nosy you are," he said. Emily smiled.

"Well then, you should have not made that statement. Who is she?"

"The one that birthed me." Basil sighed.

"Your mother?"

"No, Fady," he said sarcastically. Emily narrowed her gaze at him. He smiled. For the first time he smiled at her. *The sky must be falling,* Emily thought to herself.

"Basil!"

"Yes, my mother."

"What did she do?"

"She won't rest until she finds me a bride." He could not believe he was even talking to Emily about his mother. He had never opened up to her about anything.

"Oh my." Emily laughed a little. "The idea of arranged marriage sounds terrible to me."

"The idea of marriage itself is just terrible."

"What? You don't want to get married?"

"Not really."

"Why?"

"It's not for me."

"How?" Emily just could not understand why he did not want to get married. What was wrong with marriage? But then again it was Basil. He was a peculiar man.

"You ask a lot of questions," said Basil.

"I know." Emily laughed a little. "I am just trying to understand why you do not want to get married. Who doesn't want to get married?"

"What's the point of it?"

"Marrying the person you love."

"Love?"

"So now you will say you do not believe in love," she said.

"As a matter of fact I do not," he replied.

"What?"

"Why are we even discussing my life right now? You should be making me coffee."

Emily rolled her eyes. "You are so demanding," she said. She took a cup out of a cupboard and poured the coffee in the mug. She put sugar and milk in it.

"That is not how I drink it," Basil said to Emily.

"That is how you will drink it today." She handed him the coffee and returned to her seat and to her coffee.

"This is why I say women are too difficult." Basil took a sip of his coffee.

"We aren't difficult, it's just you that frustrates us."

"Look who is talking."

"What? I frustrate you?" Emily laughed sarcastically. "That is crazy talk. What have I done to you?"

"You are always on my case. You nag too much." Basil walked slowly towards his seat.

"You turned me into a nag. I never was one." Emily switched her laptop on. Basil just grunted in response. For some reason, she was not annoying him that day. That was the longest they had ever spoken to each other. He found himself easily talking to her about himself, it was odd how natural it was.

He watched Emily drinking her coffee and looking at the paperwork that was on the table. Her caramel skin had a nice glow to it. Her curly hair was tied up into a high ponytail. Her brown eyebrows were nicely shaped. She was not bad looking. Suddenly she turned her head and they made eye contact. Even though he had been caught staring, he did not look away.

"What?" she asked.

"What?" he asked as if he did not know what she was asking him about. Emily narrowed her gaze at him.

"So if you studied engineering, why aren't you working in the oil business?" Emily asked him.

"More questions?" he said.

"Basil, just answer the question."

He raised his eyebrows. She was so feisty and he found it fascinating. "I am just not interested," he said. Emily opened her mouth to speak but Basil beat her to it. "Then why did I study it?"

Emily laughed. He had read her mind. "Yes, why?" she said.

"That was what the sheikh wanted."

"Why do you refer to him as the sheikh?"

"Because he is a sheikh, or would you rather I call him the king?"

"No, just dad or father."

"Emily, you are too curious."

That was the first time he had ever referred to her by her first name. He never said her name. He just said what he needed to say to her without saying her name or even being polite. Emily was also shocked at how long they had spoken and about his personal life too. She was seeing a different side to him. A better side than she had been seeing.

Chapter 12

"Where is Basil?" Fady asked Emily as she walked into his office a week later. He had summoned her to his office to update her on the Magenta Oils deal.

"I do not know," Emily replied to him. She really wanted to tell him that he should be the one to tell her where Basil was. After all it was his brother. "I have not seen him all day," she added as she joined Fady at the sofas in his office.

"He has not come in again?"

"No sir, he has not."

Fady closed his eyes momentarily. He knew that his brother did not like working or being in the company. He had stayed well clear of the company all his life. However this was a different situation. His title was on the line. Fady expected Basil to rise to the occasion. He was disappointed that his brother hadn't been coming into work. In the last week it had gotten worse. He rarely came in.

"That child," said Fady.

"Sir?" Emily said.

"My brother, he is so irresponsible and lazy. I expected him to do better."

"He did well at the meeting with Magenta Oils," Emily said.

"That was one occasion, what has he done since?"

"To be fair there isn't that much to do. We are just waiting to hear back from them," she defended him. She did not think, she just spoke. After she heard herself say the words, she wondered why she was defending him. Fady was right. He was saying things that she had been saying all along.

"Are you and my brother finally getting along?" Fady asked

"Not really, why do you ask?"

"Because you are defending him."

"I am not defending him," Emily quickly said. She scratched the back of her neck awkwardly. "Just saying the truth." Her voice drifted off. Fady laughed.

"I must say that I am shocked. The two of you are getting along quicker than expected."

"We are not getting along! He is still very rude and lazy. He comes and goes as he pleases. He's a stubborn spoiled prince!" Emily spat out defensively. Her eyes widened when she realized that she said too much, in front of Basil's brother too, her boss.

He surprised her by bursting into laughter. "That was the reaction I was expecting," he said. Emily frowned slightly. She did not expect him to laugh at all.

"You are not angry at me for speaking ill of your brother?" Emily asked.

"Not at all." Fady still laughed a little. He cleared his throat. "The reason I wanted to speak to the two of you is because the terms of the Magenta Oils contract have changed," he said.

"To what?"

"They need 400 barrels of methane instead of 200."

"What?" Emily's eyes widened. "Four hundred? Why? That is too much."

"I agree. It is too much in such a short time frame."

"But why did they change it? Two hundred was a lot to begin with, especially on a new well."

"I guess their demand has increased. Also they are getting approached by more buyers."

Emily was starting to panic about the deal. She was not sure whether they could provide 400 barrels. There was only a week left. It did not make sense that they would change the terms now, but anyway the terms made were verbal. Of course they could change their minds. Buyers always changed their minds and Emily was well aware of it.

Suddenly the door opened and Basil walked into the room. Both Emily and Fady looked at Basil as he walked in. He strolled in, looking rather relaxed. He joined them at the sofas. "What is happening?" he asked them.

"Nice of you to join us," said Fady. Basil flashed him a mischievous grin.

"What did I miss?" Basil asked.

"Emily wants to kill you," Fady joked. He had caught Emily looking at Basil from the corner of her eye.

"No, I do not," Emily quickly denied it.

"She always wants to," said Basil

"That is not true."

"Emily, you always want to."

There it was again, Basil had called her by her name. She felt butterflies in her stomach. She tried to suppress the feeling but it was impossible. Fortunately, Fady started speaking about the methane project.

"I was just pulling her leg," said Fady. "Magenta Oils have decided to double up the required amount of barrels."

Basil looked surprised. "The deadline is only in a week," he said.

"That is what they have decided. Will the well pump enough?"

"I am not sure."

"There is almost nothing we can do really," said Emily. She was already feeling defensive, which was unlike her. She had given the project all she had. At this point she was not sure what she could do.

"I agree but we should try to come up with something," said Fady.

"We have worked so hard on this project, we cannot afford to lose this deal," said Emily.

"A lot is at stake," Fady agreed.

"I am going to head back to my office. I will report to you if I think of something," said Emily as she stood up. Fady nodded. Emily walked out of his office and headed back to hers.

"Father called me to check on the progress of the project," said Fady after Emily had left the office. Basil looked so uninterested.

"I bet it was our mother that called and he just spouted something in the background," said Basil. Fady laughed.

"That is exactly what happened," he said. Basil rose to his feet.

"I am off."

"You are not curious about what she had to say?"

"No."

Basil stalked to the exit. He knew that his mother had called about Basil's marriage. She had no choice but to contact Fady, since Basil was not answering her calls. He also knew that their father wanted to know whether Basil was excelling in the project. He doubted that he was. He was the irresponsible son who never amounted to anything. Basil already knew what his parents spoke to Fady about and he had no interest in discussing it. There was no need to do so.

Chapter 13

Emily headed out of Fady's office and back to the one that she shared with Basil to collect her bag. She and Fady had just been trying to figure out some options. They were not going to be able to produce 400 barrels in the short time they had left. Emily walked into the shared office. Just being in there reminded her of Basil. Of course it would, they had worked together for the past three months. She especially remembered the last time they were in the office together. He had opened up to her. It was nice. For once she was not arguing with him and he was not being rude.

She had learned a lot about him that day. She found out that he did not believe in love and did not want to get married. It was odd to her because she wanted to get married and she believed in love. She might not have been so lucky in the past, but she still had hope. She was young, there was no rush. Emily just took her bag and walked out of the office.

When Emily walked into her house, she found her grandmother in there cooking. "Nana!" Emily shouted as she walked into the kitchen.

"Why are you shouting like that? You scared me," said her grandmother with her hand on her heart.

"Why are you in my house? How did you even get in?"

"With my key, of course."

Emily stared at her nana with a blank facial expression. She shook her head and sat down at the kitchen table. "I thought I had taken that key back," she said.

"I had two made at the time," she replied. Emily shook her head.

"You are aging in a crazy way," Emily teased her. Her grandmother hit her on the head with a wooden spoon. "Ouch!" Emily screamed out.

"Wash your hands and chop the onions."

"Yes, Nana." Emily got up and did as she was told. "But, Nana, this is creepy. Please warn me beforehand when you are coming over and only use your key in emergency situations."

"I missed you, isn't that an emergency?"

"No, it isn't! I saw you on Sunday."

Her nana laughed. "Ah, guess who I saw today?" she asked as she mixed the peppers with the mushrooms in the pan.

"Who?" Emily asked flatly.

"That prince from the country club."

"What?" Emily turned sharply and looked at her grandmother. "Where did you see him?"

"I knew there was something between the two of you. Look how you are reacting from hearing that I saw him."

Emily frowned. "It's not like that, Nana. He just hasn't been at work."

"So you miss him?"

"No, I don't. There is just an important situation at work and he needs to be in," she said. She felt her cheeks heat up.

"So why are you turning red?" her nana asked.

"I am not."

"You are."

Emily sighed heavily. She started explaining the situation to her grandmother about how she was working with him on the methane project. She explained to her how important it was and what was at stake. She was only concerned about Basil's whereabouts because he had not been at work when it was urgent.

"I did not know he was that irresponsible. He sounded like a decent guy when I spoke to him," said her nana.

"You spoke to him? Why didn't you say that earlier?"

"Because you did not let me get there."

"Well what did you speak about? How did you even end up speaking to him?"

"I met him at the country club."

"You go there too often."

"It is a great social platform. I might catch you a nice-looking man." Her nana winked at her. Emily burst out laughing.

"Oh lord," she said as she laughed.

"Do you want you to hear the rest of the story or not?"

"Yes, please continue," said Emily.

"He was sitting with some older businessmen," said her nana.

"Businessmen? How do you know?"

"From the way they were dressed. Anyway I recognized him and so I greeted him."

"Oh no, just why?" Emily buried her head in her hands.

"Why not? He was very polite to me and I even invited him over for dinner," she said. Emily dropped the knife and looked at her grandmother as if she was going to have a heart attack.

"WHAT?" Emily shouted at the top of her lungs. "No way, no, he cannot come here," she added. What was her grandmother thinking by inviting Basil over? The project was to be over in a few days and she was not going to see him again, or at least have any business with him. That was how she wanted it. Why was her grandmother speaking to him and inviting him for dinner?

"Not here, but at my house," her nana said.

"But still…"

"Oh, you are so uptight. That is why you are still single."

"Nana!"

Her grandmother just laughed. Emily was not keen on the idea of her grandmother and Basil having dinner together.

Chapter 14

Basil showed up at the office just a day before the meeting with Magenta Oils. The last time Emily had seen him was in Fady's office, when he had come in late. She had been so worried about the deal. There was no way they were going to be able to provide the amount of methane required. To make matters worse, Basil had not been coming into work.

"I know that look," Basil said as he walked into their office. Emily was looking at him with an angry face. He knew that she was going to scold him for being absent and then coming in late.

"Basil, you must be tired of being a prince," Emily said to him.

"What?"

"You know full well what is at stake here. If this deal is unsuccessful, it will be horrible, I would hate it but everything will revert back to normal for me. However your father will strip you of your title."

"Okay?" Basil was not sure what she was going on about.

"This affects you the most and yet you still play around. What is wrong with you?" Emily said. Basil started walking towards Emily with a blank facial expression.

"I am aware of that. However I am not playing around," he said to her.

"Where have you been all week?"

"I had matters to attend to."

"Attending to your multiple lovers?"

Basil could not help but laugh at her. Emily frowned at him. She was all serious and he was laughing. "Basil, why are you laughing right now?" she asked him.

"I do not have multiple lovers," he said gently.

"You expect me to believe that?"

"Why is that hard to believe?"

"I know your type." Emily shook her head. "That is not the point! I do not care what you do in your spare time."

"So why did you bring it up?" Basil stopped right in front of Emily.

"Because you are never at work and... why are you standing so close to me right now?" She was angry at him and wanted to speak her mind. She wanted to scold him but he was making it difficult. Why was he standing so close to her, looking at her like that? It was distracting.

"Is it bothering you?"

"Yes, it is bothering me. I am trying to have a serious conversation here. We have the meeting tomorrow and not enough methane. That is what I wanted to talk to you about four days ago but you were nowhere to be found," Emily said to him.

"I came in to specifically talk to you about that."

"What good will that do now? The meeting is tomorrow and—" Emily was just going off on Basil, he did not even have a chance to speak. He had important information to tell her but she kept talking. He decided to cut her off by kissing her. It was the only way he could shut her up and he actually wanted to kiss her. There was something about her being feisty that turned him on.

This time Emily did not fight Basil. She let him kiss her so passionately and softly. She had not known how much she had missed his lips until he kissed her. She immediately felt butterflies in her stomach. Basil broke off the passionate kiss and pressed a small soft kiss on her lips. She stood there for a moment without saying anything.

"You can open your eyes now," Basil teased. Realization sunk in and Emily opened her eyes.

"What are you kissing me for?" she yelled out. Basil laughed.

"Because you would not stop talking." That and the fact that he really wanted to kiss her. Her lips were always tempting him and her being feisty was appealing to him.

"And the last time?" Emily asked him. Basil just shrugged his shoulders. He was not about to explain himself to her.

"Are you calm now? Can we talk?" Basil sat on the table and folded his arms over his chest.

"What do you want to talk about?"

"Look at your rosy cheeks," Basil pointed out. Emily's cheeks were still red from the kissing and being shy. Emily touched her cheeks.

"They're not red. Hey! Just tell me what it is you wanted to speak about," she snapped when she felt how warm her cheeks were. Basil laughed.

"Okay, calm down. I will tell you," he said. "The reason I have not been around so much is because I have been meeting with Natural Gasses Limited."

Emily looked surprised. "Who are they?" she asked him.

"A natural gas company. They're still new, hence that's why you do not know them."

"Okay, so why are you meeting with them in such a crucial time?"

"Because I think it will be a good investment."

Emily stared at him blankly. She was not understanding his point. "Basil, please make sense," she said to him.

"The point is I bought methane from them and we can use that for the Magenta Oils deal," he said. Emily raised her eyebrows.

"What? How did you even think of that?"

"Methane is more abundant in the ocean floor than in the ground. I knew that it would not be easy. So I researched on other companies just in case we needed emergency methane," he said. Emily stared at him with her eyes widened. She had not even thought of that. She was used to dealing with oil.

"That was good thinking on your part" she said with her hand on her heart. "But you came off as this lazy, unmotivated, irresponsible jerk."

"Thanks," he said sarcastically. Emily laughed.

"Well, you rarely came into work and then when you were here, you left early."

"The office life is not for me."

"You are just spoiled, that's all."

Basil whipped his head closer to hers. "You realize that I am a prince, right?" he said.

"And so?"

"You must treat me like one."

"After three months you still don't know me," said Emily. Basil rose to his feet. He raised her chin with his index finger.

"I know what I need to," he said. He turned on his heel and headed towards the door.

"What? Where are you going?"

"To see Fady."

"Yes, you should do that! He was looking for you all week. You are going to be in trouble." Emily wanted to see Fady yell at Basil.

"No, I am not. My brother never yells at me. Our father always blamed him for spoiling me."

"I blame him too."

Basil smiled at her and walked out of the office.

Chapter 15

It was finally time for the meeting with Magenta Oils, where they were going to sign a contract with Tadros Oil. It was the day that Fady, Basil and their father had been waiting for. The project had not been easy but they had gotten through it. Fady was particularly proud of his younger brother. He had worried for him that their father really would strip him of his title and take away all his allowances.

"You are here," Emily said to Basil as he entered the conference room dressed in his designer charcoal-gray suit and navy blue shirt. His jet-black hair had been trimmed a little and his beard was about a day old. He looked impressive. He stood next to Emily. Fady was speaking to the lawyers. They were waiting for the Magenta Oils people to come.

"Of course I am here," he replied.

"On time too."

"After the million messages you sent me last night and this morning. How did you even get my number?"

"I have my ways," said Emily with a cheeky grin on her face. She hated that she had never been able to reach him when it mattered. So the day before, she asked Fady for his number. As embarrassing as it was, it was vital.

"Now I must change it," he teased.

"After today I will not need it anyway."

"What are you two whispering about?" Fady asked Emily and Basil as he approached them.

"Nothing important," said Basil. Fady smiled and gripped his shoulder.

"Are you ready? This is the easy part."

"I am."

"I am so proud of you for getting this far. The two of you."

"Thank you," said Emily cheerfully. Basil raised his eyebrow at her. She was goofy sometimes. Rachel walked into the conference room with the Magenta Oils business men and lawyers.

Fady immediately greeted them. Mr. Johns was among the men. He was happy to see Basil and Fady. He had always respected their father and so he liked them too. They all sat down at the table. The lawyers already had the contracts. What was left, was for them to be signed.

"I am glad you were able to meet our demands, even though we changed them last minute," said Mr. Johns. Emily wanted to let him know how hard it had been, but of course that was not professional. They all had had a hard time with the sudden change in methane amount. Surprisingly it was Basil that saved the day.

"In the future we will be able to meet your demands. Please continue to do business with us," said Basil. Mr. Johns nodded.

"You take after your father," he said. Basil did not know whether to smile or not. He had never been compared to his father. Growing up, he and his father never got along because he did not want to work in the oil business. His father pushed him to do it but he refused. He just went to the university, got his degree, and just wanted to enjoy his life without any responsibilities.

Finally the contract signing began. There were two contracts, one for each company. Fady and Basil signed both copies. Mr. Johns and his business partners did the same. Tadros Oil was to deliver methane to Magenta Oils monthly for the next 10 years.

"We look forward to doing business with you," said Mr. Johns. He shook both Fady's and Basil's hands before he and his business partners and lawyers left.

"We did it!" Emily cried out after all the Magenta Oils people had left. Basil and Fady turned to look at her. She immediately felt awkward. She cleared her throat and looked down.

"We did," said Fady. He chuckled a little and tapped her shoulder. "You put a lot of effort in. Well done."

"She's so weird," said Basil referring to Emily. Fady started speaking in Arabic to Basil. Emily could not understand them, so she just watched. When Fady was done talking, he tapped Emily's shoulder and left the room. The Tadros Oil lawyers had also left the conference room.

"His highness was telling you how proud he was?" Emily asked Basil.

"Whose highness?" Basil asked.

"Your brother."

"So you call him his highness but not me?"

"Basil, let it go."

"He was telling me how proud he was and that I did well." Basil grabbed Emily's waist. Her eyes widened and she let out a squeal.

"Let me go!" she cried out.

"I could not have done it without you." He picked her up and embraced her. Emily hit him a few times and begged him to put her down but he didn't. She wrapped her arms around his neck.

"I already know that it was all because of my hard work," she joked and hugged him tightly. He too held her tightly for a moment before he put her down.

"Now I can leave this place. I have worked too hard. I need a vacation," he said. Emily frowned at him. She was about to comment on that when she suddenly remembered a pressing issue that she wanted to ask him about.

"Basil, you met my grandmother at the country club?" she asked him. All of a sudden he had a mischievous look on his face.

"Nice lady," he said.

"You're not seriously going to go for dinner, right?"

"Why not?"

"Just why would you go? You barely know her."

"She was very polite to invite me, why would I not go?"

Emily narrowed her gaze. "She wouldn't take no for answer, would she?" she asked him.

"No," said Basil. Emily knew her grandmother would be like that.

"But why were you at the country club?" she asked him.

"Meeting with the board members of Natural Gasses Limited."

"At the country club?"

"I am not cut out for the office."

Emily knew that to be true. He could barely stay in the office for more than four hours in a day.

"After all of this, and especially because of the result of this meeting, I am considering the methane business," he said.

"Eh?" Emily was shocked. "You, working?"

"Have some faith in me, woman!"

Emily started laughing. "So what you are saying is that working with me got you interested. I inspired you?" she said.

"No," he replied. Sadly she was right. Seeing how hard she worked and seeing her results inspired him. When they had started working together, he looked into her educational background and all the work she had done at their company. He wanted to know who he was working with, since there was a lot at stake for him. Since he found out that she was good at her job, he did not mind leaving her to do everything and just slacking off. That was how it started, and then he slowly got interested.

The fact that they had successfully negotiated the contract and achieved all their goals despite a few mishaps exhilarated Basil. It made him want to do it again.

"Deny it all you want," Emily said cheekily.

"Emily, don't flatter yourself."

Emily laughed. "Well, in the end everything worked out all thanks to you." She pushed him playfully. "So you will be starting here or what?" she asked as she placed her hands on her hips.

"I will buy Natural Gasses Limited."

"What? You want to buy it?"

"Yes." He had not thought too much about it. All he knew was that he wanted to buy it. He had a history of being too impulsive and that did not always work in his favor.

"That is a risky move," she said.

"You don't think I should?"

"No, I think you should." Emily was seeing a different side to him, a more mature and responsible one. "But before you should, you should check out the wells first. Don't buy something that will not benefit you or the company in the future. Find out as much information as you can about their wells," she continued. Basil nodded.

"I will," he said. As he was standing with Emily, he realized that she had been with him every step of the way. Though she nagged him, disliked him, refused to make him coffee, she had helped him a lot. He had also found himself opening up to her so easily. He never usually opened up to people. It was odd that with Emily it was easy.

"But won't you return to Al-Bisha where your bride is waiting?" Emily asked before she started giggling. Basil narrowed his eyes. There was the sarcasm and the goofiness too. He stroked her cheek with his index finger.

"Aren't you too interested in my love life?" he asked her. She whacked his hand away.

"Who is interested?"

"Last time you accused me of having multiple lovers."

"Well, you must have multiple lovers. Otherwise who were you always messaging on your phone?"

"See, you are interested."

"Goodbye," she said. She tried to walk out but Basil blocked her path. "What are you doing? I have work to do."

"Look how red your face is."

"It's not red!" she snapped, even though she could feel it heating up. It annoyed her how much she turned red around him.

"Yes it is," he said.

"Shut up!" she said and pushed him out of the way. Basil laughed loudly to annoy her as she left the room. He liked seeing her blushing around him. It showed him just how much he affected her. It was even more adorable to see her getting defensive because of it.

Chapter 16

Emily heard her phone vibrate. She growled as she rolled on her side to see who it was. She was just about to sleep. She picked up and unlocked the screen. It was a text from Basil. She wondered why he was messaging her.

What are you doing? the message read. Emily wondered why he was messaging her. She was contemplating not replying. She ended up waiting a few minutes before she replied.

Sleeping, who is this? she replied. Even though she knew full well who it was, she still asked since she had told him that she was not going to need his number after the meeting.

That message was not meant for you—

Emily frowned. Was he trying to text one of his lovers and accidentally sent it to her? It annoyed her. She wanted to just ignore him and not reply but then another message came in.

What do you mean who is this? I am sure you know full well who this is.

Emily giggled to herself. She flipped open her laptop that was on the nightstand and started browsing the internet. She wanted to leave him hanging. She felt like a teenager again, the excitement of getting a text message from a guy and playing all hard to get. She so badly wanted to message him back instantly but she waited.

Basil was a complicated man. When she thought of him, she felt different kinds of feelings. She started off disliking him. He was just pretentious and rude. He still was but kissing him had left her thinking about him often and wanting to kiss him again. There were moments when they got along but they had argued more than they had gotten along.

I do not have this number saved. Why would I know who it is? Emily messaged after about half an hour. She giggled as she waited for a reply.

I see you like to play games, Miss Gibson.

It's midnight, I have no time for games.

Hmmm.

Hmmm...?

Emily waited for a reply until she fell asleep.

***

Emily was grateful as the weekend approached, and soon it was Sunday again. The day Emily loved and hated the most in the week. After church, Emily and her family all returned to their grandmother's house. The older women went to the kitchen to start cooking immediately. Emily watched television with her brothers and her cousin Mathew.

A little later on when the food was ready, Emily's mother came to the living room where her children and nephew were. "Emily, you go set the table," she said as she walked into the room. Emily did not even hear her. She was too focused on the television. Her mother tapped Emily on the shoulder.

"Huh." Emily snapped out of her thoughts and turned around.

"I said set the table. You should be in the kitchen with the other women," her mother said and frowned at Emily.

Emily grinned. "Okay, Mom," she said and deliberately avoided commenting on her mother's statement. She was always trying to get out of doing any chores.

"Don't be sarcastic," her mother said and tried to hit her playfully but Emily was smart enough to run off. She went to the dining room and started setting the table. Her aunt brought in different dishes one by one. Suddenly the doorbell rang.

"Someone get that," Emily shouted to her brothers. She was not willing to go get it. Moments later, her brothers walked into the dining room. "Who was it?" Emily asked as she set the cutlery.

"It's just me," she heard a very familiar voice speak. She looked up and saw Basil standing there. He was dressed in casual navy blue trousers and a white polo shirt. Emily's mouth hung open. What was he doing there? She knew that her grandmother had invited him over for dinner but she did not think it was going to be at their weekly Sunday lunch.

"What are you doing here?" she asked him.

Basil was seeing a different Emily. She was wearing a knee-length pencil dress with a pattern on it. Her long curly hair was not tied up nor was it straightened. She wore it down and it actually suited her. It made her face look rounder and more adorable.

"Emily, don't be rude," her grandmother said as she walked into the room. She smiled at Basil and greeted him. She told him to sit down and make himself comfortable. He nodded and did as told. The rest of Emily's family sat down.

"This is Prince Basil, he works with our Emily," said her grandmother.

"Ohhh," Emily's brothers and cousin chorused.

"So you are *the* Basil," said Jake.

"You know of me?" Basil asked softly.

"A little," Jake replied with a smirk on his face. Emily closed her eyes from the embarrassment. She had planned not to be there when her grandmother and Basil had dinner. However it had not worked out because her grandmother was too sneaky. She refused to tell Emily when the dinner was going to be, and had invited him over without telling anyone. Her grandmother was always trying to find her a boyfriend because she felt that it was time for Emily to marry. She was already 24 years old. She should at least have been in a committed relationship.

As they were eating, Emily's brothers and cousin were analyzing Basil's every move. It did not surprise Emily that they were like that. Growing up, her brothers and Mathew were so overprotective when it came to Emily. She was younger than them and she was the only girl.

"Which country are you from?" Mathew asked Basil.

"Al-Bisha," Basil replied.

"This food must be different from what you eat in the palace," said Sandy.

"It is different in a good way. It's quite delightful and rich in flavor," said Basil with a smile on his face. Emily shook her head in amazement. He was being so polite and smiley. He was not like that to her when they had first met and he still was not like that to her.

"Are you seeing my daughter?" Emily's mother asked Basil. Emily almost choked on her juice.

"No, he isn't, Mom. We are just working together," she defended herself.

"Look her cheeks turning red," Mathew pointed out.

"My cheeks aren't red," Emily snapped. She just wanted to die of embarrassment.

"Emily has a crush," said Sandy. She smiled as she placed her hand on her heart. Emily's family teased her for a little while and laughed at her. Basil barely reacted, he just smiled. Emily just wanted the ground to open up and swallow her.

"Even though you seem like a nice guy, you have to treat Emily well. It doesn't matter whether you work together or if you are dating," said Jake.

And there it was! Emily was expecting her brothers to say something like that. "Please stop talking," she said to him but it was pointless. James and Mathew joined in the conversation. Basil agreed politely.

When they were finished eating, Emily was thankful that Basil left straight away. She made sure to walk him to his car. "Why did you not tell me that you were coming?" she asked him as they walked out of the house.

"How would I tell you?" he asked her.

"Text message or phone call."

"You expect me to communicate with you when you pretend not to have my number?"

"Huh? What are you talking about?" Emily tried to pretend as though she did not know what he was speaking about but she started smiling.

"You can't even lie with a straight face," he said to her.

"Well, why were you messaging me at night?"

"It was not meant for you."

"For one of your lovers then?"

"I am not even going to answer that question."

Emily smiled and looked up. The weather was great. It was nice and sunny. There was a cool breeze. She loved summer days. Basil turned to say something to her and found her looking at the sky with a goofy look on her face.

"What are you so happy about?" he asked her.

"The weather is great today," she replied.

"That's it?" Simple things made her happy.

"Yes, that's it." She looked at him. He was staring at her with a blank facial expression. "Go home," she said to him. Basil laughed and he walked off. He crossed the street to where his car was.

Chapter 17

The next day was very busy for Emily. She had left her house thinking she was going to work as normal but that was not the case. Basil had come to pick her up. "How did you know where I live?" she had asked him. He told her that he had gotten her address from work.

The whole day, they had spent going to meetings with Natural Gasses Limited and seeing their wells. Basil had said that Emily was the only person who knew about him wanting to buy the company. So he needed her to come with him. Emily was surprised but she happily accompanied him. It had been a long and exhausting day for her but strangely she had enjoyed it. She was now glad to be back home and in her bed. Before she closed her eyes, her phone vibrated.

What are you doing? read the message. It was from Basil.

Was this meant for me? she replied.

I can detect your sarcasm in the message.

Detect what you want. Why are you messaging me at night?

So you know who it is now?

I might.

What size are you?

Size for what? And why are you asking me that?

Answer me.

No.

Must be extra-large.

Go away!

Emily was tired but apparently not too tired to be messaging Basil. She stayed up talking to him. Of course he teased her and was rude to her in the messages. It was what he did. She was curious as to why he had asked for her size. Did she seem big to him? She wore medium dress size, and her waist was small. He must like extra-small women.

***

Basil woke up just around noon the following day. He had been messaging Emily until 5 a.m. He could not stop messaging her. Even though they had spent the day together, he still wanted to speak to her. He enjoyed teasing her. She always reacted to him. She never knew when he was serious and when he was joking. It was adorable. He also strangely found himself ignoring messages from other females. He never focused on one woman, it was unlike him. He had even stopped dating altogether.

Basil got out of bed and went to take a shower. As he was coming out of the shower, a knock sounded on the door. He wiped his hair as he went to answer it. His jaw dropped open when he opened the door and saw his mother with a small security detail. She was standing there in her traditional djellaba, a long-sleeved Arabic dress. It was made of turquoise silk and it had silver embroidery on the chest. Her jet-black hair was styled into a beehive. She wore diamond earrings.

"Mother?" said Basil. He was so shocked to see her.

"Are you just going to stand there looking at me or will you let me in?" she asked him.

"Sure, come in."

His mother gracefully walked into his deluxe suite. She sat on one of the comfortable expensive sofas.

"I will go change," said Basil as he quickly disappeared to the bedroom. He pulled on a polo shirt and a pair of shorts. He rushed back into the living room, where his mother waited for his return. "So what brings you by?" he asked her.

"Since you were not reciprocating my calls, I had no choice but to come," she replied.

"That is because I do not wish to discuss my marriage."

"You could still call me to see how I am. I see you still have not even greeted me properly."

Basil stood up and approached her. "I apologize for my impertinence," he said before he kissed her on both cheeks. He sat down next to her. "I trust that you have been well," he said.

"I have. Congratulations on being successful on your project. Your brother told me all about it."

"Yes, well, I am grateful it is over."

She stroked his cheek before she slapped him. He flinched at the sudden impact. "Your father was serious this time. I do not want you to be stripped of your title. You must come to your senses, Basil," she said to him.

"Mother, that slap hurt," he complained.

"Good! I was attempting to smack some senses into you." She sighed. "You are a 26-year-old man. You should be married. Come back with me so that we can start looking for your bride."

"I do not want a bride."

"In order to keep your father off your back, come back and work with him. You also need to be married."

"I am not going to do any of those things." Basil rose to his feet. "Let's have lunch." He held his hand out for her. She took his hand and rose to her feet too.

"At least call your father and let him know how the project went."

"I am sure Fady has already told him all about it." Basil was not bothered to call his father. They never got along. They saw things differently, which made them argue constantly.

Basil and his mother headed out of his hotel room. They went to the hotel's restaurant on the rooftop. The weather was just right for dining outside. A waiter greeted them and escorted them to a table.

"Are you seeing anyone?" his mother asked as they were looking at the menu.

"No, I am not," he replied lazily. Coincidentally, his phone vibrated. He pulled his phone out and looked at the message. A little smile tugged at his lips when he saw that the message was from Emily. *"Falling asleep at work,"* it read.

"Then who is making you smile right now?"

"Mother, I am not with anyone."

"That is strange, since you always had a female companion or two in Al-Bisha." His mother frowned. She never approved of it. Basil laughed in response.

"Well, none at the moment."

It's your fault for staying awake for so long, he replied to Emily and sent the message.

"You need to stop that. This is why I insist on you getting married. I don't want incidents like the last with Ms. Omar to happen again," she said.

Ms. Omar was the ex-wife of the minister of defense. A photograph of her speaking to Basil was taken and printed in the tabloids. They were only talking but the media suggested that they were seeing each other, especially since Basil had a history of being photographed with different women. The story soon turned into a big scandal, one which was not good for the royal family or the minister of defense.

"That isn't my fault that people twist things," said Basil.

"It was because of your history that this happened. That is why you have to turn over a new leaf."

Basil looked at his phone. Emily had replied, *I was not the one that messaged first.*

Leave work early tomorrow, he replied

Why?

Just do it.

No, I have a job and need to do my work.

I'll have the car pick you up at 2 p.m. and I'll tell Fady that you are leaving early.

Why? To go where?

"Who do you keep messaging?" Basil's mother asked. He cleared his throat and put the phone down.

"Nobody," he replied.

Chapter 18

"It isn't that amusing," Basil said to Fady, who was laughing uncontrollably.

"See, this is why you should have called her back when I told you," Fady replied. He found it hilarious that their mother had surprised him like that.

"It did not mean that she had to fly all over just to speak with me."

Before Fady could reply, there was a knock on the door. Rachel opened the door and walked in. "Sorry to disturb, but your father is on line 1," she said to Fady. He nodded and dismissed her.

"Enjoy that phone call," said Basil.

"No, you are not leaving," said Fady. He answered the phone and put it on loudspeaker. "Your majesty, I trust that you have been well. I am here with Basil," he said. Basil frowned at him. He had wanted to walk out of the room so that he did not have to speak to their father but Fady spoiled that plan.

"Basil is there?" said the sheikh in his husky voice.

"I am here, Father," said Basil.

"What are you still doing in Dallas? You should have returned when the contract was signed."

It was so typical of their father to issue demands. He had not even properly greeted either one of his sons, especially Basil whom he had not spoken to since he left Al-Bisha. They did not have the best relationship but he could still say hello.

"I am not yet ready to return," said Basil.

"Why not? You are worrying your mother. You need to return with her and find a wife."

"But, Father, I do not want to get married."

"Until when will you live your life like this? You want to play around and drag our name through the mud. I will not have it! You may have been successful with the contract, but I can still revoke your title at any time." It was clear that their father was getting angry.

"Father, please recant your anger," said Fady.

"I blame you for never reprimanding your brother. You are always supporting him and letting him make bad choices."

"Father, I am a grown man. I do not need Fady to father me," said Basil. He too was getting a little angry with his father. His father's controlling nature caused him to stray.

"Then act like a grown man! Come home immediately." The sheikh hung up the phone.

"Basil," said Fady.

"I will go when I am ready. Father wants me to return so that I can be where he can control me and force me into marriage," Basil said as he rose to his feet. A little voice inside of him reminded him that if he returned, he would not be able to see Emily. That did not sit well with him. Their relationship or whatever they had was a crazy one. He could not even explain it but it had grown to mean a lot to him. He walked out of Fady's office and headed down the hall.

Basil reached Emily's office a few moments later. He opened the door without knocking. She was sitting at her desk when he walked in. She looked very shocked to see him. "What are you doing here?" she asked him.

"I told you to leave work early today," he said flatly.

"And I told you that I had work."

"Fady knows you have to leave early. Let's go,"

Emily raised her eyebrow. "And just what exactly did you tell him?" she asked him. Basil shrugged his shoulders.

"That you need to leave early," he said. Emily still sat in her chair without any intentions of getting up. "Emily, let's go," he said. She laughed a little.

"No, I don't even know where we are going and why," she said.

"If you do not stand up, then I will pick you up."

Emily knew that he was not bluffing. Last time he had picked her up when she tried to block the door. She stood up instantly and tidied up her desk. She picked up her bag and walked to Basil. "Fine," she said. He opened the door and let her walk out first. Emily walked skeptically. He had never opened the door for her. He always walked through first and never held it for her.

"Look at you being a gentleman today," she said.

"I know, being in this place has sadly changed me," he replied. Emily laughed but Basil didn't.

"But what is wrong with you today?"

"What do you mean?"

"You seem down."

"I am not."

"But you are."

Basil was a little bit surprised that she was able to see it. The two of them walked out of the building. His car was already waiting for them. "My parents," he said as he opened the door for her. She got into the car, and he got in afterwards.

"What about your parents?" Emily asked him when they were in the car and driving off.

"My mother decided to drop by yesterday."

"What? She came to Dallas?"

"Yes."

"Isn't that a good thing?"

Basil told her why his mother came. Then he told her about his earlier conversation with his father. Emily was surprised to learn that he did not want to return Al-Bisha. She thought that he was going to return after the project. Emily took his hands into hers. She did not know why she did it. It just came natural to her. Basil looked at her.

"After you buy Natural Gasses Limited, what then?" she asked him.

"Since my family has been trying to get into the methane business, it will be easier with this new company. We will now be in charge of their wells and methane. I could stay here and manage the methane projects," he replied. Emily smiled.

"In three months, you have matured."

"However, my father wants me to return. He still threatens to strip me of my title."

"Can you live without your title and allowances?"

"Of course, I will just move in with your nana. I am sure she will be happy to have me around."

"You do not want to be around my family. You've seen them, they're crazy."

"But you sit and eat together. We do not do that." Obviously they did not. Everyone had their chambers and could dine alone. They also had different commitments, so they did not dine together often. When they did, it was rather formal. Basil did not know Emily's family but he felt warm around them. They argued and teased Emily, but it was all for fun. It was clear that they got along and were very close. He strangely felt at home. And the food was really good. It was just everything that he hadn't experienced at the palace.

"Yeah, I guess," she said. Sometimes her family was too much to deal with. They were always so nosy.

"You do not know how lucky you are."

The driver suddenly parked. They were in the town center. They both got out of the car. Basil led Emily into a very expensive boutique. She knew that place. She had always walked past it because of how expensive it was. She did not dare to go in.

"Why are we here?" she asked Basil.

"To update your wardrobe, of course," he replied. Emily's jaw hung open. That was why he asked for her size.

"There is nothing wrong with my wardrobe!" she protested.

"I still remember the outfit you were wearing when we first met."

Emily raised her eyebrows. "The one you ruined?" she said.

"I was not even the one driving," he defended himself. They started arguing so heatedly about the incident that they did not realize that the sales consultant was standing in front of them. Emily looked at her and cleared her throat.

"Sorry about that," she apologized.

"It is okay, how can I help?" she replied.

"Can you show us everything in her size?" Basil asked.

"I don't need anything," said Emily. Basil scanned her from head to toe.

"You do."

Emily frowned at him. The sales consultant smiled and asked them to follow her. She showed them different outfits that would suit Emily's hourglass figure.

"We will get them all," said Basil.

"Wow, your husband is very generous," said the sales consultant.

"We are not married," Basil and Emily chorused.

"Oh, excuse me. You just make a good couple, that is all." She quickly bagged up the clothes. Basil handed her his credit card. She swiped the card and then asked him to sign for the payment. She then handed the card back to him.

"Be a good husband and carry the bags," said Emily sarcastically. She thanked the woman and walked off. Basil had no choice but to carry the bags. Emily was giggling to herself as she walked out. She knew that he was going to complain about carrying the bags, since he was a prince and all.

And he did just that when they got back in the car. The driver was also surprised to see Basil carrying all the bags. He quickly took them from Basil and put them in the trunk.

Chapter 18

Fady stood in the doorway of the hotel feeling rather confused. He was to have lunch with Basil and their mother, however they were arguing when he walked in. "What did I just walk into?" Fady asked. Their mother handed him the tablet. He looked at the screen and saw pictures of Basil and Emily.

"That's Emily," he said.

"You know her," said their mother.

"She works for Tadros Oil. She was the one working Basil on the methane project," he said. He looked down at the tablet and read the article. It was from Al-Bisha and was suggesting that Emily and Basil were in a relationship. "Well, we know that tabloids always make things up," he said and looked at Basil for an explanation.

"And so why was he buying clothes with her?" their mother asked. There were pictures from when they had gone to the boutique and other pictures from different days, at lunch and when they were going for meetings.

"I bought them for her," Basil replied.

"Did you?" Fady looked shocked. "You never buy anyone clothes."

"Your father is not happy. At least be seen with a woman of standards," said their mother. Basil was a prince of Al-Bisha. He needed to be with a woman from a reputable background.

"Standards?" Basil repeated.

"Her parents are divorced and they're from the lower class."

"You already did a background check on her?"

"You know that information never comes into my hands before everything has been checked out."

Basil was feeling a little bit furious. Emily did not deserve that. "Her family is just fine," he said.

"Is she the reason why you refuse to return and marry?"

"I have never showed interest in marriage. This has nothing to do with Emily."

Fady stood there trying grasp the situation. Had his brother and Emily gone from arguing to dating? When had that happened? "Are you seeing Emily?" he asked.

"Isn't it obvious? Anyway he will get bored of her soon," said their mother.

"I will not," said Basil. Their mother's phone started ringing. She fished it out of her purse.

"It's your father," she said before she answered it. "Hello... okay," she pressed a button on the phone. "You are now on loudspeaker," she said to the sheikh.

"Basil, I have had it with you. Every time I open the newspaper, there is something about you," said the sheikh. He was already heated up. Basil was not shocked that their father was angry. Of course he did not approve of Emily. They needed Basil to make a marriage that would benefit the royal family. It could not be just any woman. Then there was the fact that Basil had been photographed with many women, he had the playboy image. For an Arabic man, that brought dishonor to the family.

"Father, please calm down. It is not good for your heart," said Fady.

"Basil, make a decision right now; get on the jet with your mother in the next half an hour or stay there and be stripped of your title."

"Father, he already accomplished the task you gave him. You said you would not strip him of his title if he did that."

"Fady, stay out of this. He only accomplished one little thing."

"I did more than that with the help of the woman you speak so little of," said Basil.

"Respect your father," said their mother.

"Did you know that I just bought Natural Gasses Limited, a small methane company?"

"What are you talking about?" said Fady.

"Since you wanted to get into the methane business, I bought this company that has some viable wells that will be good for the growth of Tadros Oil. Anyway here is my decision, you can keep my title and the money," Basil said. He fished his wallet out of his pocket and placed it on the table before he walked out of the hotel. His mother and Fady called out after him but he did not respond.

Three months ago, he would have looked for a way to keep his title. However now he was not going to do so. He wanted to be with Emily. He wanted to enjoy the Sunday lunches with her family, something his family never did. Her family had showed him what a real family should look like. He was tired of his controlling father. He did not want to marry the woman his mother chose for him. That was not the life he wanted.

"What are you doing here?" Emily asked Basil when she opened her front door and found him standing there. She noticed that he looked down again. "What happened? Come in," she said to him. He just walked into her house and hugged her. She wrapped her arms around him and rubbed his back. They went to sit at the sofas. Emily asked him what had happened. He told her everything.

"I told you that I might have to move in with your nana," he joked but with no smile on his face.

"You can stay here. I mean it's a one-bedroom house, so you will have to sleep on the sofa. It's no palace but you can stay here."

"I bet your nana would give me a bed."

Emily frowned. "I can't understand when and how you and I got this cozy." she said.

"I have my ways," he said and pulled her into his arms. He stroked her face with the back of his hand.

"You won't regret it?"

"I won't."

"Are you sure?"

"I am sure."

"Sure sure?"

"Sure sure." Basil felt like a child repeating after her.

"Pinky swear." Emily stuck her small finger out. Basil smiled and stuck his out too. They linked their fingers and pinky swore. She was so goofy, adorable, sarcastic, feisty, and smart. Those were her best qualities. Emily giggled and held Basil's face in her hands and then kissed him. Basil wrapped his arms around her and kissed her back.

***

A month had passed since Basil had last seen his mother and spoken to his father. Fady had come to Emily's house to ask about Basil's whereabouts and fortunately found him there. Fady tried to get Basil to reconsider his decision but he was not willing to give Emily up. Fady always had his brother's best interest at heart, so he supported his decision. He tried to give Basil money, but he refused it.

In that month, Basil had lived life in a different way from what he had known. It was nice to be around Emily and her family. He got to know all of them more, and he liked what he learned. Whenever he was around them, they did not treat him like a prince. He was just a normal man to them. On one Sunday, they had their Sunday lunch at Emily's house. They always rotated among Emily's grandmother, mother, aunt, and herself.

There was a knock on Emily's door. Mathew went to answer the door and returned with three unfamiliar guests. Emily only recognized Fady. Basil was in the middle of a conversation with Emily's grandmother when he looked up and saw his parents. It did not shock him that his mother had come, but it was shocking to see the sheikh. The older, still handsome man stood tall next to his wife. He wore an expensive suit.

"Hello, son," said the sheikh in husky voice. Emily sprung to her feet immediately.

"Hello, Father," Basil replied. His mother approached him and touched his face.

"I have missed you," she said to him. "Come home." She had not expected for him to stand firm with his decision for so long.

"Not without Emily," he replied.

"We should give them privacy," said Emily. She gestured for her family to follow her out. They had all been standing there staring.

"We need to talk to you as well, Miss Gibson," said the sheikh.

"Me?" Emily swallowed nervously. The sheikh nodded. Her family had to leave the house and wait outside, since her house was not big enough.

"I have come all this way to reinstate your title," the sheikh said to Basil. "And to meet the woman that makes you want to live as a normal man."

Emily shifted uncomfortably. It was not like the sheikh was a rich businessman or a sheikh of a village. He was the king of Al-Bisha and he was in her tiny house. It was a little bit intimidating.

"We would like to get to know you, and invite you to Al-Bisha with us," said the queen. "You have changed our lacking son for the better, and Fady speaks highly of you also."

"I did not change Basil. He just found himself," said Emily.

"Let's compromise," said Fady. "How about he runs all the methane projects, since he was the one to buy the methane company? When he marries, he will move back to Al-Bisha," he continued.

"As long as it is Emily I marry."

"Huh, what?" Emily's eyes flew open. Her heart started pounding really fast. She felt her cheeks turn red. She could not believe her ears. Had he just said he wanted to marry her?

"I am not leaving this place without you," said Basil.

"But you were so against marriage."

"I am not against marrying you."

Emily burst out laughing in response. She scratched the back of her neck. "So you are saying that you love me?" she said. She knew that he did not believe in love, so he would need help saying it. Basil grunted and shifted awkwardly.

"Something like that," he said.

"Tadros men are useless when it comes to romance," said the queen. All three Tadros men looked at her. She gently patted her low bun and looked away. Emily laughed.

"I do love you Emily and want to marry you," said Basil.

"Say yes!" Emily's grandmother shouted from outside the front door before Emily could answer.

"Nana, you are ruining the moment and shouldn't be listening!" Emily shouted back. She shook her head. She was not surprised her family had been eavesdropping. Basil's mother laughed.

"Say yes, Emily," his mother said to her.

"Yes, I will marry you," she said with red cheeks and a smile on her face. Of course she would marry him. Her heart beat for him more than it had ever done for any man. In the last month, she had gotten to really know him. She had spent every single day with him and could not imagine living without him. Her family opened the door cheering. They too had fallen in love with Basil and wanted him to be a part of the family.

What to read next?

If you liked this book, you will also like *In Love with a Haunted House*. Another interesting book is *The Sheikh's Unofficial Bodyguard*.

In Love With a Haunted House

The last thing Mallory Clark wants to do is move back home. She has no choice, though, since the company she worked for in Chicago has just downsized her, and everybody else. To make matters worse her fiancé has broken their engagement, and her heart, leaving her hurting and scarred. When her mother tells her that the house she always coveted as a child, the once-famed Gray Oaks Manor, is not only on the market but selling for a song, it seems to Mallory that the best thing she could possibly do would be to put Chicago, and everything and everyone in it, behind her. Arriving back home she runs into gorgeous and mysterious Blake Hunter. Blake is new to town and like her he is interested in buying the crumbling old Victorian on the edge of the historic downtown center, although his reasons are his own. Blake is instantly intrigued by the flame-haired beauty with the fiery temper and the vulnerable expression in her eyes. He can feel the attraction between them and knows it is mutual, but he also knows that the last thing on earth he needs is to get involved with a woman determined to take away a house he has to have.

The Sheikh's Unofficial Bodyguard

Despite a very awkward job interview, Emma is hired as a receptionist at Besada Oils Corporation. Sheikh Kiro Besada manages his father's oil business in Dallas and after a few encounters with Emma, he thinks that she is odd but intriguing. One day a few men in masks ambush Kiro in a company parking lot and put him in their minivan. Emma sees this from her car, calls the police and blocks the exit so the attackers can't get away. Kiro realizes that Emma is not only intriguing but also brave, and she affects his heart in a way no other woman has. Emma and Kiro realize that despite their very different characters they are slowly but steadily falling in love with each other. During a trip to Kiro's home country they face many challenges that may either split them apart or make their relationship even stronger.

About Kate Goldman

In childhood I observed a huge love between my mother and father and promised myself that one day I would meet a man whom I would fall in love with head over heels. At the age of 16, I wrote my first romance story that was published in a student magazine and was read by my entire neighborhood. I enjoy writing romance stories that readers can turn into captivating imaginary movies where characters fall in love, overcome difficult obstacles, and participate in best adventures of their lives. Most of the time you can find me reading a great fiction book in a cozy armchair, writing a romance story in a hammock near the ocean, or traveling around the world with my beloved husband.

One Last Thing…

If you believe that *The Oil Prince i*s worth sharing, would you spend a minute to let your friends know about it?

If this book lets them have a great time, they will be enormously grateful to you – as will I.

Kate

www.KateGoldmanBooks.com

Made in the USA
Coppell, TX
22 November 2023